CRADLED

BOOK FIVE OF THE BEHOLDER SERIES

CHRISTINA BAUER

COPYRIGHT

Monster House Books
Brighton, MA 02135
ISBN 9781946677303
First Edition

CONTENTS

DEDICATION

For All Those Who Kick Ass, Take Names
And Read Books

CRADLED

*T*ap…tap…tap…

Someone was wearing out their knuckles on my bedroom door. Yanking my covers over my head, I tried blocking out the sound. It didn't work.

Tap…tap…tap…

I stifled a groan. Most days, I'd say this about my life: *It's good to be the queen.* Sadly, today wasn't one of those days. Last night, I'd asked the castle servants not to disturb me until dawn. Now I lay in bed, trying to rest, and yet?

Tap…tap…tap…

Whoever it was, they weren't giving up.

I opened my eyes a crack, finding myself alone in bed. My husband wasn't here, but that was no surprise. Rowan knew I wanted to sleep in, so he'd slipped off a while ago. As for my bedchamber, the place looked as it always did. The red stone walls were lined with tapestries of animals being magickally brought to life by mages. My own spell books lay in neat piles on a nearby table.

Peering through the chamber's window holes, the outside world looked dark. *Definitely not morning.* There could only be one explanation; the staff must have missed my orders to sleep in.

"Please return later," I called. "At dawn."

A muffled voice echoed through the closed door. "It's long past dawn. The sun came up more than twelve hours ago."

The speaker was Jicho, my little brother in law. "Are you toying with me?" Jicho loved his practical jokes.

"Not at all. It's nine o'clock at night. The Fete of the Family has already started. Rowan's been there for hours."

Sitting up, I carefully scanned the view from my window. Sure enough, the moon peeped over the sill.

Whoa.

That was unexpected, not to mention concerning. Rowan's people were Creation Casters, mages who gained magick from life. I'd been trained as a Necromancer, so my mage powers were drawn from the echoes of existence in bones. Together, we'd been ruling both classes of magick users for a year now, and I'd learned one thing early on.

Creation Casters loved their festivals. A lot.

Rowan and I tried to attend as many celebrations as passible, and Fete of the Family was one of the biggest. Not one that I wanted to miss. After pushing off my covers, I set my bare feet on the cold marble floor. "I'll join you soon."

In this case, *soon* meant after I had a warm bath and some hot food. Caster parties lasted all night. No doubt, there was still plenty of time to join the fun.

"No, you need to hurry." Jicho lowered his voice to a hush. "I've had a vision."

My breath caught. Although he was only ten years old, Jicho was a powerful Seer who often had painfully accurate visions of the future. That said, he was also a mischievous imp. For instance, last week Jicho claimed he had a vision that the castle would implode if he had to do his lessons.

Needless to say, Jicho still finished his lessons; the castle did not implode.

I stood up, pulled on a cloak, and opened the door. Jicho stood in the outer hallway, all tanned skin, gangly limbs and knobby knees in his toga-style Seer robes. His head was shaved in the style for Seer mages. By contrast, I was tall and slender with pale skin and long dark hair.

Jicho didn't look up as I motioned him inside. *Interesting.* When it came to Jicho, lack of eye contact was a classic but common sign.

The boy might be up something.

"Why don't you come in and explain about your vision?" I asked.

"Uh, no." Jicho kicked at the floor with his sandal. "I need to get back to the party." He kept avoiding my line of sight. That settled it.

The boy was definitely *up to something.*

I folded my arms over my chest. "Tell me about this vision of yours first."

"It wasn't exactly a vision." Now Jicho stared at the vaulted ceiling as if the cobwebs were beyond fascinating.

A chill crawled up my neck. *Not exactly a vision?* That could only mean one thing. I set my fists on my hips. "Have you been playing in gateways again?"

Gateways were arches of stone that magickally connected our world to other realms. Rowan and I were unusual in that we could share our Creation Caster and Necromancer magick, combining it into hybrid power. By mixing our energies, we gave all our spells an extra boost. Hybrid magick meant that my husband and I had enough energy to open gateways. For a while, we were the only mages who could.

Until Jicho.

As the boy grew, Jicho was turning into a Seer who wielded unbelievable levels of magick. About a month ago, he figured out how to open gateways. Not good.

Jicho shot me a gap-toothed smile. "Did I open a gateway? Depends on how you define gateways."

His big grin always made me melt a little. That said, I worked hard to keep my features stern. Playing around with gateways was serious stuff.

"Don't try to charm your way out of this one." I wagged my finger at him. "Answer my question. This new vision of yours—did you get it from a gateway, yes or no?"

"Yes, but only a little bit?" Jicho blinked his big green eyes at me while holding his thumb and forefinger an inch apart. He had long lashes, just like Rowan. It was getting harder not to visibly melt under his charm.

Even so, I kept up my serious stare. "You know it's forbidden to open random gateways." I shook my head. "You could let in any kind of monster or disease. Even worse, you could get stuck in another world and then, how would we find you?"

Jicho puffed out his lower lip. "But I only peep into the gateways; I don't go inside them. Plus, gateways show me totally different futures than my visions do. It's really important that I learn how to use them."

"No gateways, Jicho."

"Well, I already saw this vision in the gateway." His voice lowered to a hush. "Something big is coming."

I lifted my brows. *Something big?* The last time Jicho used those words, he went on to predict a massive Tsunami along our southern coast. Thanks to his warning, we were able to evacuate the local population. Even so, it was an incredibly close call. If we hadn't acted quickly to transport everyone inland, thousands would have died.

I used Jicho's own words back at him. "Define big."

"I'm not sure." Jicho waved his hands around. "The vision is a little foggy. But I see warriors with strange helmets...And they're definitely at the Fete of the Family."

My skin prickled over with gooseflesh. Unknown warriors? Rowan and I had heard no reports of insurrection, so that left only one power with enough resources to mount an army against us. *The Royals.* But that was unlikely; we'd recently signed a treaty with them. In exchange for us mages providing magickal services, the Royals promised to protect us if we were ever attacked. The fact that the Royals were the only ones with enough resources to attack us wasn't necessarily spelled out in the treaty, but we all knew why we were signing it.

So who was left to assault us with a professional army? An image of a gateway appeared in my mind. If Jicho somehow left one of those archways open, anyone could pass through and cause trouble.

Then there was the matter of my parents: two mages who'd spent eons opening and powering gateways, mostly by draining the magick inherent in their own children. Rowan and I had sent them into exile. We hadn't heard anything from them since.

Were they the ones returning with warriors to fight us? My stomach sank. It was certainly possible.

"That does sound rather serious," I said. "I'll join the fete right away."

Jicho exhaled. "Good, I'll let Rowan know." As the boy raced off down the hallway, his words echoed through my mind.

Warriors. Something big.

A weight of worry settled onto my shoulders. I may not be a Seer, but my mage senses still said that whatever was coming, it would be far worse than a Tsunami. Taking in a deep breath, I steeled my shoulders. No matter what was about to strike, I had my husband and people to fight at my side. Together, we could face down any enemy.

I hoped.

2

As I stood in my white nightshift, my sleepy mind processed two key pieces of news. First, Jicho had peeked into a gateway, where he'd seen strange warriors at our Fete of the Family celebration. And second, despite the fact that I slept the entire day, I still wanted to do nothing but crawl back into bed.

That wasn't like me. Not one bit.

Perhaps I was ill.

I worried my lip with my teeth. There was no question that I needed to visit the fete as soon as possible. But what if I were so sick that I couldn't cast properly? That wasn't something I wanted to find out in front of a crowd, especially if that crowd turned out to be an invading army.

Nodding once to myself, I made my decision. Before

I left my bedchamber, I would cast a spell for a wellness skull. If there were anything to worry about, then a wellness skull would tell me the truth and quickly.

Time to cast.

Closing my eyes, I reached out with my mage senses. I spent years at the Zelle Cloister learning how to wield my Necromancer powers, so the process came easily. The first step in any Necromancer spell was always to find some bones.

Simple enough.

Rowan and I owned a number of castles across our realm. This particular one, called Jiwe La Moto, was surrounded by dense jungle. When most people thought of a rainforest, they pictured greenery. In reality however, jungles were filled with far more bones than leaves.

Using my mage powers, I now scanned through the layers of skeletons under the grounds nearby. Images of bones and their past lives appeared in my mind. I saw bird skulls that were still filled with the lost echoes of joyful songs. Next I detected the skeletons of monkeys long gone. Even in death, their love for their jungle home—as well as each other—radiated out into the world. *So beautiful.* I tapped into that energy, pulling it into my body.

As the magick streamed inside me, the bones in my

left hand glowed blue. Power ricocheted around my chest as I spoke the incantation.

> *"Bones and time*
> *Still and chime*
> *I seek the wellness spell*
> *A monkey skull to tell"*

A moment later, a sphere of shifting light congealed in the air before me. Within seconds, the orb solidified into the form of a monkey skull. The head hovered in the air, immobile. Within it, every tooth and bone gleamed with light and power. The skull shifted to face me straight on.

"What do you seek, Grand Mistress?"

Now I had many titles. Tsarina of the Necromancers and Genesis Regina of the Creation Casters were the two that were used most often. That said, my favorite was still Grand Mistress Necromancer. I'd spent five long years honing my skills to reach that level, and I never tired of hearing the title.

"Please check me for any illness," I said.

"As you command." Like most wellness skulls, this one had a refined way of speaking. These skulls came loaded with medical information and, as such, not a small amount of attitude.

Little by little, the monkey skull opened its mouth. Instantly, dozens of orbs of multicolored light sped out from its jaws.

I gasped. *What a lovely spell.*

Once they were free, the bright spheres raced around me in overlapping corkscrew patterns. The movement reminded me of ribbons around a maypole. The lights pulsed with brightness before zooming back inside the skull's mouth. The monkey's head floated in the air before me for a long moment, its eye holes narrowing in thought.

"You aren't ill," said the skull.

My shoulders relaxed; I hadn't even realized that I'd bunched up my muscles with worry. "Thank you." As I spoke, I couldn't help but smile. "You are dismissed."

"But there's more to tell you," it added.

I tilted my head. "Oh?" Usually, wellness skulls only said if something was wrong and then disappeared. They never offered extra information.

"Go on," I said.

When the skull spoke, every word seemed to move so slowly, it was as if the head were enchanted by a slowness spell. "You are pregnant, Grand Mistress."

On reflex, I pulled on my ear. "I must have heard you incorrectly. It sounded as if you said that I'm pregnant."

The skull glowed more brightly. "I did, Grand

Mistress. You're one month along in your pregnancy, to be precise."

I scrubbed my hands over my face. Rowan and I weren't planning on having a family, ever. *There had to me some mistake.* "But I'd cast spells against this."

"They didn't work," said the skull simply. "Mortals like you are, at best, an imperfect form of life. I'd speculate that you made a mistake in your casting."

I shot the skull a dry look. "Thank you for that assessment." Those are the words that came from my mouth, but what I was thinking was something along the lines of:

No.

Just no.

The hovering skull lifted its chin. "I'll take my leave now."

"Thank you," I said. "You may go."

There was a burst of light as the wellness skull disappeared from the room. For a long moment, I could only stare at the spot where it had been suspended. I hugged my elbows.

Pregnant. I was really pregnant. No wonder I had been feeling so tired.

Lacing my fingers behind my neck, I tried to process this news. It wasn't easy. There were good reasons why I'd cast spells to avoid pregnancy. Both Rowan and I had too many evil branches in our respective family trees. To begin with, there were my parents, who'd spent thousands of years draining their own children in order to power gateways to other realms...all so they could rule those different worlds. Then, there was my brother Viktor, who tried to kill every last mage in the land. His goal? To oust my parents from power so he could usurp their rule. Now Viktor was dead and my parents were in exile through a random gateway.

Good riddance.

Rowan's family wasn't much better, though. It's true that my husband's father was a kind man and strong warrior, but Rowan's mother Zoriah? That woman gave a new and fouler definition to the word *evil*. Even though my parents ultimately saw their children as supernatural fuel, they still treated us with kindness and respect. That wasn't true for Zoriah. She spent every waking moment attacking her offspring in some form or another. It was arguable that she turned Rowan's older brother Shujaa into a homicidal maniac. Needless to say, many in the realm slept better now that both Shujaa and Zoriah were dead. I certainly did.

I set my palms flat against my belly. Hopefully, our child would inherit the best of me and Rowan. In the meantime? I may have my answers about my health, but I still had questions about potential warriors invading our Fete of the Family. I needed to give Rowan the news about my pregnancy, too. If I rushed, we'd have a chance to talk before Jicho's vision came to pass.

No time to lose.

I quickly pulled on a set of Caster leathers: fitted pants and a matching jacket. They were light and comfortable. Not exactly formal regal dress, but Casters appreciated it when Rowan and I dressed as common folk every once in a while. Opening the door, I then stepped off into the outer hallway. It wouldn't take me long to reach the celebration...and face whatever fate Jicho's vision might bring.

3

With quick steps, I made my way through the castle. Red stone surrounded me everywhere: walls, floors, even large vases were made of the stuff. It's what made Jiwe La Moto my favorite of our castles. With so much stone, the place reminded me of my old Cloister, the Zelle, a compound that had been carved right out of a mountainside.

I soon stepped out of the castle and onto the large open space behind it. Or, to be accurate, it was as open as things got this deep in the jungle. Tall palm trees dotted the clearing. Heavy ropes of vines looped between them. Humidity tinged the air. All that was to be expected. But the moment I walked outside, I noticed something rather odd.

There was no music.

No dancing.

No joyful chatter from partygoers.

By this time of night, a Caster celebration would resemble a happy and somewhat drunken mob scene. Instead, our people lurked under palm trees, gripping untouched mugs of ale.

So strange.

I scanned the clearing carefully. Why was everyone so somber? Had Jicho's mystery warriors already arrived? By the thin beams of moonlight, I couldn't make out any fighters in strange helms, but I did discover the reason for the lack of fun at this particular festival.

Zoriah's relatives had joined the party.

Rowan's mother Zoriah had not been a pleasant woman; her family followed suit. Zoriah's relatives were all Seers, supposedly powerful, but with very little in the way of actual magick. Zoriah was the only one with strong Seer abilities. Still, lack of magickal skill didn't stop Zoriah's family from acting as if they were superior to everyone else.

All in all, no one could wreck a party better than Rowan's Seer relatives. They simply meandered around between groups, delivering back-handed complements until everyone's mood was ruined. I recalled a few of their classic comments in my direction.

Why Elea, you look so much cleaner today! But perhaps that's because you aren't wearing those horrible Necromancer robes.

How brave of you to exile your parents! I never would have faced down gods for fear that they'd retaliate on me and everyone I loved.

And my personal favorite...

We will never attend a party with those horrible Necromancer death lovers. How do you ever stand being around them?

They really were awful people. I was working on a few ways to blunt their ability to ruin festivals, but such things took time and interest. I didn't have much of either when it came to Zoriah's family. Plus, they weren't the only ones with worries about spending time with Necromancers. We'd kept our Necromancer and Caster duties separate, trying to give our respective people time to adjust. Meanwhile, I had to find Rowan before anything major happened because, of course...

Baby.

At the thought of my pregnancy, bands of anxiety tightened around my chest. Rowan and I had repeatedly discussed how we'd never have a family. Now I was pregnant. Explaining that wouldn't be easy.

I spotted Rowan standing alone at the edge of the clearing. Moonlight outlined his muscular form; the man had limbs as thick as tree trunks. As always, my heart lightened to see the familiar lines of his face. Rowan's features were rugged and fierce, with a strong jawline and short brown hair. Like me, he wore his Caster leathers.

My Rowan.

As I approached, Rowan gave me one of his crooked smiles. It made little shocks of excitement dance across my skin. "Feeling better?" he asked.

"Much," I replied. "Thank you for the extra sleep."

"You can go back to bed if you like." Rowan pulled me into a deep hug. I melted into the warmth of his embrace. "This festival is anything but festive. You won't miss anything."

I wrapped my arms around his waist, loving the feel of solid muscle under supple leather. "I noticed our guests."

"Yes, my mother's side of the family are horrible." Rowan's voice lowered to a growl. "Their presence here does nothing but remind me why we vowed to never become parents. Why risk bringing anyone like *them* into the world?" He leaned back until his emerald gaze locked with mine. "Am I right?"

I opened my mouth, ready to respond. No words came out.

What do I say here?

Yes, we did agree to that, but now I'm pregnant anyway. Surprise!

Once more I tried to force out the words. Silence. Then Jicho approached, his eyes alight with excitement. He tugged on my wrist and in all honesty, I'd never been happier for an interruption.

"I saw more things in the gatew—" Jicho cleared his throat. "I mean, I just had some new visions."

Rowan broke our embrace and focused on his little brother. "You told me you were going to see Elea."

Jicho raised his pointer finger. "I did see Elea. Woke her up and everything."

"Ah." Rowan considered this for a moment. "But then, did you activate a gateway as well?"

"Maybe just a little." Like before, Jicho held his pointer finger and thumb an inch apart.

Rowan shook his head. "Jicho."

Now that I'd had a few moments to catch my breath, I felt ready to explain to Rowan about my pregnancy. "Jicho," I said. "Your brother and I were just talking. Could give us a min—"

"But I saw the man who's coming." Jicho pulled on my sleeve again. "He's about to arrive right there!" Jicho pointed to the center of the clearing.

All of a sudden, hundreds of bright spots sparkled in the center of the clearing. At first, I thought it might be lightning bugs. Then I noticed how the light was bronze in color, as well as multiplying into the general shape of an archway.

Not lightning bugs.

Tingles of anxiety moved down my spine. *Someone was opening a gateway at the Fete of the Family.*

Sure enough, an archway materialized in the clearing. Other gateways that I'd seen were made from blocks of stone, but this one was a single smooth curve of metal. Under the arch, the view to the other side of the jungle disappeared. Perfect darkness loomed under the new gateway. My limbs tightened with anticipation.

Any second now, someone would walk right through.

Could it be my parents?

Memories appeared. I recalled my father, the Sire of Souls. He always appeared so austere and pale in his dark armor. On the other hand, mother was all things golden, smiling, and soft. In this realm, the two were still worshipped Sire of Souls and The Lady of Creation. Rowan and I hadn't seen fit to tear down their temples and reorganize the mages who followed them. To so many people, my parents were wise magick users who led others on the path to mastering their own powers. It didn't feel right to destroy a belief that helped so many.

Even so, I was in no mood to see my parents again.

The pair tried to kill me; I sent them into exile. Was this the moment they returned? I set my palms against my stomach. How would this affect my unborn child?

Lights glinted under the archway. Three figures walked out. My shoulders slumped with relief. Whatever these figures were, they were shorter than me and Rowan.

Not my parents.

The figures came into clearer focus and I sucked in a shaky breath. These may not be my parents, but they didn't look friendly, either.

A man led the group. In the moonlight, I could see that he wore a top hat, short coat, vest, and cravat. A walking stick was gripped in his left hand. Small round glasses sat atop the man's nose, the lenses dark. Between the glasses and top hat, all I could see of the stranger's face was his pointed beard and long curlicue moustache. Everything about him seemed to be colored bronze, but that might have been an effect of the moonlight.

Beside him walked two metal warriors. Both were stout and compact, neither male nor female, and made entirely out of metal. Great helms covered their heads and shoulders, with built-in goggles shielding their eyes. They looked inhuman, unstoppable, and terrifying. Rowan slipped his hand around my waist, pulling me closer to him. I appreciated the warmth and comfort.

All around us, the partygoers slipped deeper into the shadows. Concern flowed out from them in waves. Still, as long as Rowan and I appeared calm, our people wouldn't panic.

Even so, I wasn't sure how long we could stay serene. There was no knowing what we were dealing with here.

The man paused before me and Rowan. "Greetings, Elea of Braddock. I am Kronos, King of Quetum." He gestured behind him. "These are my Oculus Warriors."

Up close, I could see that Kronos was made entirely out of spun wire. Dainty metal cords formed his beard and moustache. All his clothes were bronze fabric accented by thick rivets. His glasses were small, round and made of the same reflective metal. Even his skin was a delicate swirl of metal thread.

Rowan pulled me closer against him. "My wife is Tsarina of the Necromancers and Genesis Regina of the Creation Casters. Address her as such."

"So many titles." Kronos huffed out a breath through his metal nostrils. Wisps of steam curled into the heavy night air. "How impressive."

Meanwhile, Kronos seemed anything but impressed. The man clearly had an attitude against me in particular. The question was *why?*

My friend Amelia stepped out from the crowd. Rowan's brother Kade walked beside her. The two of them were what the Casters called mates, and what Necromacners called married. Kade had a hefty body, strong bone structure and intense green eyes. Essentially, he was a slightly smaller version of Rowan. Meanwhile, Amelia always reminded me of a living doll. It helped that she had a bow-shaped mouth, large eyes, and pale skin. Like always, my friend wore a frilly pink gown paired with a hoop skirt and fitted bodice.

"Greetings," Amelia waved happily at Kronos and his Oculus Warriors. "You're all machines, aren't you? Do you utilize clockwork mechanism?"

Amelia was a brilliant engineer. As she spoke, there was no missing the intelligent gleam in her eyes. I'd seen Amelia use this tactic before, mostly on Royals who brought little mechanical oddities to court. My friend was inserting herself to assess what literally made things tick.

Good work, Amelia.

"Clockwork mechanism?" repeated Kronos. More steam huffed out from his nose. "I am far more than that. You look upon machinery perfected."

"How very interesting." Amelia craned her head from side to side, a motion that made her red ringlets bounce. "By perfected, do you mean you have a magickal component?" She rolled her eyes. "What am I saying? Of course you have magick. Otherwise, how could you have opened the gateway that got you here." She pointed to the walking stick in Kronos's hand. "Oh, that's topped by a moonstone. Those are so rare in this realm and excellent for storing power. In fact, I've never even seen one that large. It must be where you keep your energy, right?"

Shifting his grip on his walking stick, Kronos completely covered the moonstone. "Machines take what is best of the flesh and perfect it. But I did not come to tutor you on such matters." He pointedly stared in my direction. "I wish to discuss your parents."

My heart sank. Somehow, I knew my evil family was behind all this. When I trained to be a Necromancer, I was taught how to hide all emotion. Now I leaned into that learning, hard. It took all my skill to keep my features level as I spoke. "What about my parents?"

"I'm here to discuss their welfare." Kronos's mouth ticked up into a mechanical smile. "You want to keep your parents happy and safe, don't you?"

The hold on my emotions snapped. My mouth fell open in a classic sign of shock. "What?"

"I suspected as much," said Kronos slowly. "You loathe them."

I could kick myself, I was so angry at showing my emotions. I'd spent too long with the Creation Casters. My ability to hide my feelings was fading. Still, there was no point in mourning past mistakes. Straightening my shoulders, I stared at Kronos head on.

"Family matters are rather personal," I said evenly. "Perhaps we should go somewhere more quiet to discuss this?"

Kronos gave a stiff half-bow. "Whatever you think best."

Rowan turned to his brother Kade. "Where do you suggest we meet?"

My clever Rowan. As Captain of the imperial guard, Kade would have scoped out every inch of Jiwe La Moto. Rowan's brother would certainly know the best spot for our meeting.

"The central feasting hall would be ideal." Kade turned to Kronos. "Allow me to lead you there and settle you in."

Amelia rushed up to Kronos's side. "I'll join you for the journey. I have plenty more questions to ask about your kind, and this will give us an opportunity to talk."

Kronos's gaze slowly shifted between me and Rowan. "Won't you walk with us?" he asked.

"Not now, but soon," I answered. "First Rowan and I must close out this event you interrupted." *And scheme together on what to do with you.*

"Your people, eh?" Kronos scanned the faint outlines of bodies around the edges of the clearing. For a moment, I thought the metal king might refuse to go, which would be problematic. Rowan and I could really use some time to plan. "Ah, I see them now. Rather tricky, aren't they?"

"Tricky isn't the word I'd use." I couldn't stop the anger from seeping into my voice. I was losing control over my emotions again. "My people have grown up in jungles and hide in them with ease. That's wisdom, not trickery."

"Be that as may," Kronos adjusted his top hat. "You shall meet me in the central feasting hall in no less than five minutes. That is my solemn order."

"Really?" Kade straightened. "I have *orders* as well." The way Rowan's brother said the word *orders*, it was clear he thought Kronos shouldn't giving any. Kade snapped his fingers. "Guards! Fall out."

A dozen Imperial Guards in Caster leathers marched forth from the shadows, forming two neat rows, one on either side of Kronos and his Oculus warriors. At the same time, Amelia swept in, wrapped her hand around Kronos's elbow and led him away.

"Tell me all about Quetum," I heard Amelia say as she stepped off into the darkness. "Do your people breathe steam? Are you made only of bronze? Can your Oculus Warriors talk?" As they walked along, Amelia kept scanning Kronos from head to toe.

I allowed myself a small smile. In the past, I'd seen Amelia use this assessment tactic before. To Kronos, she'd appear the curious innocent, asking question after question. In truth, Kronos didn't need to answer any of Amelia's queries. My friend could deduce how his mechanics worked simply by observing him in motion. Amelia said such inspections were always done best when the subject didn't realize they were being watched.

Once Kronos, Amelia, Kade, and our guards were all well and gone, I turned to address the crowd still gathered at the edges of the clearing. "My people," I called. "I hereby declare that the Fete of the Family is now officially over."

"Please return to your homes," added Rowan.

No one made a move to leave, though. Instead, hundreds of our subjects came out of the shadows to asked dozens of questions about Kronos.

"Who was that mechanical king?"

"Are we about to be invaded?"

"Should we evacuate?"

"Is this all a plot by the Necromancers."

It took some time, but Rowan and I were able to assure the partygoers that the mechanical king was harmless, no one was going to invade us, this was not Necromancer plot, and that the best thing everyone could do now was go home. Eventually—and with some gentle encouragement from more of Kade's Imperial Guards—every one did leave.

Once the party was well and truly done, Rowan leaned against the trunk of a nearby tree. After folding his arms over his chest, Rowan looked up into the foliage. "Leaving means you too, Jicho."

A familiar voice echoed in from the upper fronds. "Can't I go with you to meet with the metal man?" It was Jicho, of course. The boy was forever hiding in rafters and trees. "After all, I told you he was coming in the first place."

"What do you think?" asked Rowan.

Jicho sighed. "You'll both say I can't go."

With those words, a pair of gangly legs dangled from a nearby branch. A second later, Jicho leapt down, landing on the ground right beside us. He looked the same as before, except his red Seer robes now had bits of leaf stuck in the folds. He puffed out his lower lip. "You never let me do anything interesting."

I leveled the boy with my best maternal stare. "Parlays with strange metal kings are no place for a ten year old boy."

Jicho kicked at the ground. "Maybe."

Rowan stepped closer to his brother. "This is serious, Jicho. Promise you'll go directly to your room and stay there."

Jicho shot us both a too-wide smile. "Of course, I will."

After more than a year with Jicho, I knew that grin all too well. Along with avoiding eye contact, excessive grinning was another sure sign that Jicho was up to something. Plus, there was no question what the boy planned to do. He was exceptionally talented at avoiding his guards and sneaking out of his chambers.

That wouldn't work tonight, though.

Yesterday Rowan and I had placed dozens of new lock spells all over Jicho's chambers. Those wards should be more than enough to keep the child in his own rooms until we saw fit to let him out.

"Good night, Jicho." I said pointedly. My point being this: *time to get to your room.*

Still smiling, Jicho blew me a two-handed kiss. "Good night, lovely Elea." He then turned to Rowan and set both palms over his heart. "Sleep well, my dear brother."

"Uh huh," said Rowan.

After a final wave in our direction, Jicho skip-walked into the darkness. Once the boy was well out of earshot, Rowan turned to me. "How peeved will he be when he discovers our locking spells will keep him in his room all night?"

I let out a low whistle. "Quite peeved, I should think. He's rather convinced he'll be free to follow us."

In the distance, the lights of Jiwe La Moto blinked in the darkness. Worry tightened across my neck and shoulders. Somewhere inside that castle, a mechanical king was waiting for us.

And I still hadn't told Rowan about my pregnancy.

Although now, there were more pressing things to discuss, namely Kronos. "I think our five minutes are over," I said. "We need a plan for how to deal with this Kronos."

"I have a few ideas along those lines." Rowan raised his right hand. The veins there glowed red with power. "But first, we need to collect magick inside ourselves. Lots of magick."

"Agreed." Closing my eyes, I reached out to draw extra Necromancer power into my soul. Once both Rowan and I had enough magick, then we could plot how to uncover why Kronos was here...and then send him on his way as quickly as possible.

4

*S*econds ticked by while Rowan and I pulled more magick into our souls. As fresh energy poured into me, the bones in my left hand glowed bright blue, creating a haze of brightness that cut through the night. Beside me, the veins in Rowan's hand did the same, only with red light. As more power entered me, the cacophony of the jungle seemed to grow louder as well—buzzing insects, croaking frogs, and the ghostly cries of potoo birds.

Soon, I was so filled with magick, my soul felt ready to burst from my skin. Lowering my hand, I stopped pulling in fresh power and forced the brightness in my bones to fade. I turned to Rowan. His sturdy frame loomed beside me, looking all things fierce and powerful. His hand no longer glowed, either, so he'd finished pulling in energy as well. It was time to talk.

Stepping closer to Rowan, I was careful to speak in a low voice. "What do you think of Kronos?"

"He's not here as an invader." Rowan's voice was a low rumble. "Two warriors isn't enough."

"Agreed," I said. "He's here to scout our realm. Plan his attack, whatever that is." The moment I said *attack* out loud, the word reverberated across my nerves. My brother Viktor had all but eliminated any mage with power. If someone decided to invade us, we could be rather easily defeated.

"Not our realm," countered Rowan. "You."

My eyes widened. "Why do you say that?"

Rowan counted off his observations on his fingers. "Kronos knew your name before he arrived and took care to misspeak your title. Then he mentioned your parents, testing to confirm his suspicion that you didn't like them."

I pinched the bridge of my nose, trying to process this information. "Do you think Kronos is somehow in league with my parents?"

Rowan's intense green gaze locked with mine. "I don't know, Elea. He could be. It's too early to tell."

I scrubbed my palms over my face. "We need to see if Amelia has discovered anything about Kronos. She was assessing him as they walked away. Perhaps she's detected information that may be useful."

Rowan nodded once. "One way to find out."

We didn't require further discussion. Moving in unison, Rowan and I crossed the clearing and made our way to a back door for Jiwe La Moto. Amelia was waiting for us inside.

"Your five minutes are long over," my friend announced. "He is not happy."

No question who *he* was in this statement. *Kronos*.

Rowan tilted his head. "And what does *he* plan to do about it?"

"Cast a transfer spell to wherever you are." Amelia gestured toward me. "Or to be accurate, to wherever Elea is. You're the one he's here to see and I don't like that."

"It's not my favorite thought, either." I rested my hand on my stomach. I'd only known about my pregnancy for less than an hour, and already I was worrying how anything might affect the baby. Interacting with Kronos seemed dangerous with a capital D. "Let's hurry to the central feasting hall." I shivered. "I don't want to confront Kronos in a random corridor."

"Good thinking." Rowan leaned over and kissed the top of my head. Like always, his gentle attention made me blush. As the three of us began our march toward the central feasting hall, Rowan focused on Amelia.

"You were observing Kronos before," my husband asked. "What have you discovered?"

"Kronos is a machine who was purposely designed," answered Amelia. "Every line of that man was assembled from custom parts. He's what I call a control module." Amelia then went on to explain in detail about her theories on control modules. I wish I could say I found the conversation invigorating, but instead, my need for sleep came back with a vengeance. Before I knew it, Amelia was finishing up her speech. "Kronos is intelligent. A problem solver. He was created to monitor something mechanical and crucial to infrastructure." She tapped her chin. "Like a train crossing or a dam, something along those lines. That's the key thing."

Amelia slowed her steps and I realized that we'd turned down the access corridor for the central feasting hall. There wasn't much time left.

"What have you discovered about the Oculus Warriors?" I asked.

"Up close, they seem jammed together from spare parts or something," answered Amelia. "If Kronos is a command module, they're built to be mechanical muscle. Not a lot of brains paired with tons of brawn." She tapped chin. "As a matter of fact, I have some more books in my lab that might be helpful. I could do some quick research."

The doorway to the central feasting hall opened a few yards ahead. The three of us paused and I turned to Amelia once more. "Please check out your library," I said. "And thank you for all your help."

"Are you kidding?" Amelia set her fists on her hips. "For the record, any time mechanical people are involved, I want part of the action."

I couldn't help but smile. "Request noticed." Leaning in, I gave Amelia a quick hug. Touching was something that Necromancers discouraged, but Creation Casters expected it. To acclimate to my new role as Genesis Regina, I was trying to work embracing into more of my interactions. So far, I was good at hugging Rowan and Jicho a lot, and Amelia just a little bit. I quickly stepped back from the embrace. "Let us know what you discover."

"I will." Amelia rushed off in the direction of her lab. "Good luck." She called over her shoulder.

With Amelia gone, Rowan and I marched inside in the central feasting hall. The space was large, made of red stone, and lined with heavy tapestries. Great oak beams crisscrossed the vaulted ceiling. I frowned. This chamber was filled with shadows, even on sunny days. And all those beams overhead? They were some of

Jicho's favorite places to climb. How could I have forgotten?

I carefully scanned the oak planks above me, but it was too dark to see clearly. Had Jicho snuck into this room?

Rowan leaned in to whisper in my ear. "I'm thinking the same thing, and I don't see him." No question which *him* my husband was talking about, either. *Jicho.*

"Do you think our wards will keep him in his chambers?" I asked.

"Kade's got extra guards all over this castle," answered Rowan. "If Jicho goes anywhere, someone will notice."

Rowan made a good point. We'd seen Imperial Guards throughout our walk here. Kade had them deployed everywhere. And in this chamber, a solid line of them encircled the walls. Plus, Kade himself stood at attention just inside the doorway. Some knots of worry loosened inside me.

Kade had this under control.

In fact, the only place where guards weren't standing was before the main hearth, which was a sizable structure as tall as Rowan. A fire roared inside it. Before that fireplace, there stood Kronos, his body as still as a metal statue. Shifting flames highlighted the many cords of bronze wire that made up his body, suit, and skin.

Behind Kronos there stood his Oculus Warriors. Fire-light accented the identical goggle-like eyes of their matching helms.

As Rowan and I approached, the metal king didn't so much as flinch, let alone look over in our direction. With every step, my pulse sped. Something about this mechanical man set my nerves on edge.

Oh, yes. That would be the fact that he's here for me and— to make things more complex—I happen to be pregnant.

Rowan and I paused near the hearth.

"You wished to talk," said Rowan. "My queen and I are listening."

"Quetum is a clockwork world." Kronos's voice was a melodic tenor. "Beautiful. Precise. Imbued with purpose. As a rule, we don't allow those with corruptible flesh to enter our realm. But your parents entered my world without a plan or permission. But you knew that already, didn't you?"

The way Kronos asked the question, it was clear that the mechanical king already knew the answer.

"You sent your parents off into exile," continued Kronos. "And you didn't particularly care which planets received their, ah, magnificence." The way Kronos said the word *magnificence*, it was clear that he thought my parents were a menace.

Sadly, he was right. My parents were a menace.

Guilt settled on my shoulders. In all honesty, I hadn't considered where my parents had gone once they went into exile. Suddenly, that seemed like a rather foolish oversight. What had the Sire of Souls and the Lady of Creation done to Quetum? Nervous energy moved through me in waves. Before I knew it, I was talking again.

"We were in a battle," I said quickly. "My parents were trying to kill me. Sending them off into exile was a matter of self preservation. Life and death." The moment the words left my mouth, I wished I could take them back. Talking about my parents was making me lose control. I was here to gain information, not blab every concept that fell into my brain.

Rowan gently rested his hand on my shoulder. His touch was all things reassuring. Without saying a word, Rowan told me that everything would be all right.

We were together.

We could do this.

Reaching up, I laced my fingers with Rowan's. He gave my hand a gentle squeeze and that was all I needed to keep going. Taking in a deep breath, I refocused on Kronos. "What do you want?"

"The Sire of Souls and the Lady of Creation are criminals," said Kronos. "Your parents stole magick from the engine that runs our planet. They emptied it out entirely. In doing so, the Sire and Lady turned our beautiful and bright world into a dead clock. And once they had what they wanted, your parents went into hiding. I've been hunting them down ever since, but to no avail." He gestured sadly to his Oculus Warriors. "Even my finest fighters have come up empty."

"Hold on, now." I couldn't believe what I was hearing. "You say that my parents stole magick from your planet?" I shook my head. "That doesn't make any sense. Those two had so much magickal power, they were worshipped as deities in this realm. They didn't even need to pull in power, it simply *was* them. Why would they want to steal your energy?"

"I assume exiling them meant blocking their access to this world?" Using his walking stick, Kronos gestured around the chamber. "And if they ever wished to return, I would guess they'd need a little extra energy?"

How I hated answering these questions. "That's true," I replied.

Kronos pointed the end of the walking stick in my direction. "Touch this moonstone and willingly give me the energy your parents stole. Then, I'll be on my way."

I took a half-step backward. "You can't be serious."

"I'm as serious as a doomsday clock." Kronos jabbed the end of the stick in my direction. "This is no ordinary walking stick. It's called the Bezel Wand, and it powers the entire engine for my home planet of Quetum from the Bezel Tower. Power it up. You owe me."

Now, I hadn't been queen and tsarina for a year without learning that everyone has claims. In fact, Rowan and I sat over claims court once a month. Which peasant owns what plot of land, that kind of thing. Verbal claims were as common as raindrops and as easy to wash away with a truth spell.

"If you're telling the truth," I countered, "then it will be easy to provide us with proof to substantiate your claims. Once we have that, then we can discuss what to do next."

Kronos lifted his chin. "I don't have proof on hand. I came here to parlay in good faith."

Rowan lifted his right hand. "We can cast a spell to conjure up your evidence. I'd like to see a vision of the Sire and Lady stealing your magick."

"I refuse to debase myself with such nonsense." Kronos waggled the walking stuck—what he'd called a Bezel Wand—once more in my direction. "Touch it. Power it up." He gave me a sly smile. "Or you could try to take it from me."

All the air seemed to get pulled out from my lungs. *What game was he playing at?*

In a protective move, Rowan stepped between me

and Kronos. "Elea isn't doing anything of the kind. Leave."

"Then I'm afraid we're at an impasse." Kronos set the Bezel Wand onto the floor and rested his gloved hands atop the moonstone top.

All of a sudden, Jicho dropped down from the rafters to land beside me and Rowan. The sight of his little body in Seer robes made me gasp.

"What are you doing here?" I asked.

"I knew about the wards spells, so I never went to my rooms."

"Jicho," said Rowan in a warning tone.

"No, you have to listen," cried Jicho. "Kronos is about to cast a spell; I just saw it in a vision!"

My blood iced over with fear. Jicho's visions were rarely wrong. Looking over, I saw Kronos had gripped the middle length of his walking stick with both hands, raising it high. The moonstone atop it now gleamed with power.

Oh, no.

Jicho was right.

Kronos was about to unleash a spell.

On reflex, I gripped Rowan's hand, ready to share our magick and do a casting of our own. As his Caster energy flowed into my body, one thought overtook my mind.

Please, let this work.

What happened next took a matter of seconds, but it felt as if a slowness spell had been cast over the chamber. Kronos slammed his walking stick down onto the ground. A great wave of bronze power slowly streamed from the impact point to roll out across the floor. I'd seen that kind of casting before.

It was a transformation wave.

This kind of spell was mostly invisible, unless you knew what to look for. If you stared closely, the air would shimmer with the barest bronze light. It always reminded me of how summer heat warped the air, only with a tinge of color thrown into the mix. In reality, the atmosphere was charged with magick. And that spell would change everything it came it touch with. Already the floor around Kronos was turning bronze. There was no question what he planned to do: transform everything and person around him into metal.

In this case, that meant Rowan, Jicho, Kade and our Imperial Guards.

Not an option.

While Kronos released his spell, I gripped Rowan's hand more tightly. My husband's red Caster power mixed with my blue Necromancer energy, creating violet light that shone out from our arms and chests. Rowan and I didn't discuss what spell to cast, but then again, we didn't need to. Transformation waves had only one counter-spell. We called out the incantation in unison:

"Preserve. Hinder. Fight."

Violet light poured off our palms. A wave of energy rolled out from our bodies to meet Kronos's spell. The two castings slammed into each other, making the ground shake with the force of their contact. Kronos's spell exploded into a million tiny bits of bronze shimmer.

Kronos slammed his walking stick onto the ground again. "Contain!" he called. Instantly, the tiny bits of bronze reformed into a large metal bubble that surrounded me, Rowan, Jicho, Kronos, and his two Oculus warriors. We were imprisoned.

We couldn't run away now, even if we wanted to. Jicho gripped my waist and buryied his face against my side. "I shouldn't have come here."

When I spoke, I took care to use my most calming voice. "Everything will be fine, Jicho." After that, I looked to Rowan and said three words. "Gateway. Stone serpents."

There was no need to say more; Rowan knew exactly what I meant. He and I needed to open a gateway to

Quetum and fast. Once the portal the other world was in place, we could cast stone serpents in order to herd Kronos and his buddies right through it.

And speaking of those Oculus Warriors, the pair were now twitching and making clicking noises.

I didn't take that as a good sign.

Kronos raised his Bezel Wand above his head once again.

That was an even worse development.

Rowan gave my hand another squeeze. "Serpents first," he said. Jicho gripped my waist more tightly. The thought occurred that I had both Jicho and my baby relying on me now.

This had to work.

"Let's cast," I said.

Once again, Rowan and I didn't need many words to get in sync. Our first priority was getting that Bezel Wand out of Kronos's hands, and stone serpents should do the trick..

Still holding hands, Rowan and I released our next volley of power. Violet-colored mist sped out from our free palms. As the magick left our bodies, we spoke the spell together.

"Fang and stone,
Bring us menace full grown"

On the floor before us, the mist of our spell congealed into the form of dozens of writhing vipers. Although they moved like regular serpents, each of these snakes would be stone hard to the touch. Rowan then pointed to Kronos and the Oculus Warriors. "Serpents, bring us the walking stick. Take them all down!"

Jicho peeped up from his spot by my waist. His eyes were all-black. The veins in his neck and chest had all darkened as well. That could only mean one thing. His Seer powers were active.

"I had another vision." Jicho's voice came out with a low, dream-like quality. *"Watch for the round gateway; it will bring you the lightning goddess and her consort. They must bring fire swords to the windings. Only then will you and Rowan kill Kronos."* Jichoo blinked hard as his eyes and skin returned to normal. "But it should only be you, Rowan, the lightning goddess, and her consort. Promise me you'll remember."

"I won't forget," I said quickly. *Lightning goddess. Consort. Fire swords.* That was the kind of prophecy that stayed with you.

A chorus of hisses broke up my thoughts. Our stone serpents were now speeding across the floor, heading right toward Kronos and his Oculus Warriors. My pulse sped.

This was it. Our counterspell.

For his part, Kronos simply folded his arms across his chest and lifted his chin. I frowned.

Kronos is calm. That's unexpected.

I couldn't see past his reflective glasses, but somehow, I was certain that the mechanical king had closed his eyes. Then he moved his lips, no doubt speaking the silent words to a spell.

And he's casting again. That's ominous.

A moment later, Kronos's entire form shimmered with bronze light. All the many wires that made up his body glowed. With a series of small pops, some of the metal cords lifted up from his limbs and clothing.

I blinked. Hard.

Were the wires of Kronos's skin really popping up? Indeed, they were rising. A moment later, all the cords contorted into the same insect shape.

Spiders.

Jolts of worry moved down my back. Dozens of mechanical spiders had appeared on Kronos's body, each one as large as my palm.

I've never been squeamish about spiders, but then, I'd never encountered ones that were both mechanical and suffused with magick. Who knew what these things were capable of?

Moving together, the spiders crawled across the floor to engage our stone serpents in battle. Our snakes squeezed the spiders until they snapped, or bit the mechanical insects into useless scraps of metal. For their part, the mechanical spiders wound the serpents into heavy metal cocoons, the webbing so thick that the snakes could barely move, let alone escape. All the while, Kronos watched the battle and grinned, his metal teeth shining in the firelight.

At the same time, the Oculus Warriors had finished their own small transformation. A dozen long antennae-like metal arms swung out from each of their backs. Every thin limb was topped by a spinning metal saw blade.

My breath caught. *This was dire.* Rowan, Jicho and I were still surrounded by a bubble of bronze, so we were unable to escape. Help also didn't seem to be coming for us, either. Kronos had untold stores of magick in the moonstone atop his walking stick; Rowan and I were limited by what we could pull in, process, and transform via an incantation. Even worse, our reserves of magick were getting low. Rowan and I could probably cast one more spell before we'd need to pull in fresh power, and that took time. We'd planned for that to be a gateway spell, but the way it was looking now? We'd need to do something else entirely. I pulled Jicho closer to my side; the boy was shivering with fright.

"Transfer treasure," I said.

"Right," said Rowan. Again, we didn't need to have a long conversation. Both Rowan and I knew about the transfer treasure spell. It was a kind of shielding magick that would create a protective shell around all three of us before completing a transfer spell to someplace safe. We needed to get Jicho out of here and recharge our magick stores. Once we were full again, we could return to the fight.

Rowan nodded and gripped my hand even more tightly. Fresh power moved through us both, making our skin shine with purple brightness. We quickly spoke incantation.

"Block. Protect. Defy. Move."

Once again, our free hands lit up with violet light. Magick and mist poured from our palms onto the floor. My soul lightened. *The spell was working.* All my focus went into forcing more magick out of my being and into this final casting. It wasn't easy, considering how the Oculus Warriors were closing in. To my mind, the low hum of their circular blades became impossibly loud.

Then, something tickled my shoulder.

Looking down, I saw Jicho was covered in mechanical spiders. *Head to toe.* Some of the metal insects had crawled off and onto my shoulder, and that was what had caused the tickling sensation before. I took in a shaky breath.

Spiders. And they were biting both me and Jicho.

The insects had moved so quickly—and the Oculus Warriors had been so distracting—that I hadn't noticed the spiders were attacking until it was too late. Every muscle in my body tightened with alarm.

Rowan and I weren't done with our transfer treasure spell. That casting needed to be complete so we could protect ourselves from Kronos. However, if we didn't get these spiders off, then we'd be dead before we could transfer out of here anyway. Already, spider venom numbing my arm and shoulder.

"Rowan!" I cried.

My husband turned to me. All the color drained from his face. Even so, my husband's voice was calm as he spoke. "I see them, Elea. Stay still."

Turning, Rowan lifted his arms toward me. Fresh magick poured off both of Rowan's palms, flowing directly toward myself and Jicho. Rowan's lips moved in a low murmur as he spoke different incantations, trying to modify the transfer treasure spell so it could protect against this new attack.

Purple light surrounded me and Jicho. The brightness was harmless to us, but destructive to the spiders. The insects let off little mechanical screeches as they fell off both out bodies. The Oculus Warriors paused nearby, their metallic arms still deployed around them like some insane kind of halo.

"What's happened?" whispered Jicho. His beloved face was wild with terror. "I can't feel my arms and legs."

"Shhh," I soothed. "It's going to be fine. I promise."

I scanned the bronze bubble round us. It was solid. All our stone serpents were now wrapped up in cocoons. The Oculus Warriors were no longer attacking. Kronos stood across the room, his walking stick still gripped firmly in his hands.

"So you see," said Kronos. "I am far more powerful than you. And I now have something you want."

Before my eyes, Jicho changed. His skin became a singular shade of bronze. His warm flesh turned cold against me. One antennae arm from an Oculus Warriors shot out. At the end of that thin limb, a round saw blade still whirred. And it was only a breath away from Jicho's neck.

I still had power and magick inside me. There was no way I'd allow my Jicho to be hurt. I pushed fresh energy into my palm. Beside me, Rowan did the same.

"By all means," said Kronos. "Cast another spell if you wish to see him dead."

Before me, the Oculus Warrior's blade nicked the

skin on Jicho's neck. A single drop of bronze-colored blood dripped down his throat.

I looked to Rowan. All the rage and fear in my heart was reflected in my husband's face. I lowered my hand and stopped casting my spell. Rowan did the same.

"A wise choice." Kronos didn't order the Oculus warrior away from Jicho, but the blade didn't break the boy's skin again, either.

"I can't feel my body," whispered Jicho. "What are they doing to me?"

"You're going to be fine," I said.

"We'll figure something out," added Rowan.

"No," countered Kronos. "You'll listen to what I have to say." Kronos pointed at Jicho. Bronze light flared around the mechanical kings hand. Instantly, a line of wire shot off Kronos's finger and crossed the room, ending by looped around Jicho's wrists. Within seconds, Jicho's hands were tied together.

"Come here, lad," ordered Kronos. "Warriors, stay apace."

And Jicho began to march. With every step, the Oculus warriors kept in sync, on on either side of Jicho. And one warrior also kept that spinning saw blade right above our boy's skin.

"I'm not doing this," cried Jicho as he marched. The child was terrified. Rage boiled through me, but I held my tongue. Rowan spoke the truth. He and I would figure out a way to defeat Kronos.

Jicho stopped beside Kronos and then turned around to face us. Bronze tears streamed down his plump cheeks. On reflex, I went to reach toward Jicho, but my left arm wouldn't move. That's when I saw it. My left arm and shoulder had been turned to bronze as well.

"I understand this is all a bit of a shock," said Kronos. "So I'll give you time to process. I have the boy. You have until midnight tomorrow to come willingly to my realm and hand over your magick." He raised his Bezel Wand. "I hold all the power. Don't forget that."

Kronos raised the Bezel Wand once again and brought it down on the floor. With a flash of light, another gateway opened behind Kronos. Like the one at the Fete of the Family, this one was an archway of solid bronze. "We'll be waiting for you in the dungeons of Bezel Tower."

At those words, the Oculus Warriors instantly shut down the spinning blades on the many antennae-like arms that protruded from their backs. Together with Kronos and Jicho, they all stepped back through the gateway. With a flash of bronze light, the magickal arch disappeared. The moment Kronos was gone, the bronze bubble started melting away around us.

For a long moment, I could only stare at the spot

where the gateway had just stood. My thoughts kept reviewing everything that had happened since we reached the Fete of the Family. To begin with, there was Kronos, who was clearly involved with my parents in some way. Then I pictured the mechanical insects, Bezel Wand, and Oculus warriors. Worst of all, Kronos didn't even have his Oculus Warriors attack us—just the spinning blades were enough to distract our attention while his mechanical spiders did the rest. And now, Jicho was gone and we had less than one day to rescue him.

My sweet Jicho.

And all of this was topped by the facts that I had both a metal arm and a secret pregnancy. There wasn't time to worry about either one.

Rowan pulled me into a soft hug. I pressed my cheek against my husband's chest and allowed the tears to fall. In the end, Jicho's first vision had been right all along.

Something big had happened and more.

*a*s I took comfort in Rowan's embrace, the bronze bubble that had surrounded us slowly lowered. Within seconds, it had disappeared entirely, revealing the central feasting hall beyond. The place looked as it had before, only now the huge chamber was empty, save for Amelia and Kade. Both looked miserable.

"We saw everything that happened inside the bubble," said Amelia. "I'm so sorry about Jicho." She eyed my arm. "And you're injured."

I stepped back, breaking my embrace with Rowan. "My arm doesn't hurt," I said, rubbing my left shoulder. "It's more cold than anything. I'm sure we can cast a spell to heal it."

Kade marched over to Rowan. "We must raise an

army, open a gateway, and invade Quetum. We'll take our brother back." Pure fury blazed in Kade's green eyes. "Mark my words. We'll raze that realm to the ground."

My mouth fell open with surprise. Kade wasn't one to jump into danger without thinking. "Not so fast," I said. "We've no idea what Quetum is like. Our people could be walking into a trap."

Rowan's full mouth thinned to a determined line. "How many Caster mages are battle ready?" he asked Kade.

"You can't be serious," I said.

Rowan's gaze met mine. I'd never seen him angrier. "We'll only take volunteers," he explained. After that, my husband focused once again on Kade. "How many battle mages do we have? Thirty?"

"Perhaps fifteen," replied Kade. "There are far more battle ready Necromancers."

"Good point." Rowan turned to me once more. "We need to transport to the Zelle Cloister. Talk to your second in command there, Quinn. If you ask as their Tsarina, you'll get plenty of volunteers."

I took a half-step backward. "I'm not asking for anything right now."

"How can you say that?" Rowan's voice deepened with held-in rage. "This is Jicho."

"No one loves Jicho more than I do," I explained. The

moment the words left my lips, I knew they were true. "We have different ways of fighting for him. Before the battle with Kronos ended, Jicho had another vision. He gave me specific instructions on how to save him."

The harsh line of Rowan's mouth softened a little. "What did he tell you?"

Closing my eyes, I recalled the exact words to Jicho's vision. I spoke the prophecy aloud:

"Watch for the round gateway; it will bring you the lightning goddess and her consort. They must bring fire swords to the windings. Only then can you and Rowan kill Kronos."

"So nothing about armies or invasions," said Rowan.

"Jicho was very specific," I explained. "It was only to be you, me, the lightning goddess, and her consort who would go to Quetum. That's all."

Rowan rubbed his neck. "Watch for a round gateway. What do you think that means?"

"I'm not sure." I began to absently braid by long dark hair. It was someone I often did when thinking things through. "If it means that we sit around and wait for a gateway to open, then that's not going to happen. We need to cast a gateway spell to open another world and then a summoning incantation for the lightning goddess. That way, the gateway will open onto wherever the lightning goddess may be."

"Agreed." Rowan gestured toward my arm. "Of course, we need to heal your arm before doing anything."

Kade paced a nervous line nearby. "I'd still prefer that we raise an army."

"I disagree," said Amelia. Stepping to Kade's side, she set her hand onto his elbow. Kade instantly stopped pacing. A little of the sadness inside me ebbed away. Kade was a quiet one, but that firm exterior hid an inner turmoil of emotions. Amelia could always calm him.

"What are you thinking, my love?" asked Kade.

"We need our army here," explained Amelia. "No doubt, rumors are already spreading across the country-side. Too many people saw Kronos at the celebration last night."

"She's right," I said. "That's what took us so long to leave the celebration. The partygoers had lots of questions. They weren't happy."

"I see what you mean," said Kade. "Half the realm could be in a panic by midday."

Amelia nodded. "The Imperial family must be visibly seen as competent and in control." She glanced around the feasting hall, her eyes lost in thought. "I've got it. Let's hold a military parade through the major cities.

The people love those. It will distract everyone from rumors of Kronos while giving Elea and Rowan time to act."

Kade leaned in until his forehead gently touched Amelia's. "You're a brilliant woman, you know that?"

Amelia's face flushed. "Just wait until you hear my ideas for mage fireworks that will end the parade."

"Can't wait," said Kade.

With that, the two made their goodbyes and headed off to organize what would certainly become the finest parade and firework celebration in history. With that in store, I couldn't imagine our people worrying about Kronos, or wondering where Rowan, Jicho and I had disappeared to, either.

With Amelia and Kade gone, I returned my attention to Rowan. My husband had already pulled fresh magick into his body. The veins in his right hand glowed red with power. His gaze locked onto my metal arm.

"May I?" he asked.

There was no question what Rowan wanted to do here: heal my arm. The limb in question was now itching like crazy, so I couldn't be happier with this suggestion.

"Please do," I said.

Stepping closer, Rowan set his palms on my metal

arm. His voice was a low rumble as he spoke a healing incantation.

"Heal. Strife. Comfort. Life."

At those words, crimson brightness flared out from under Rowan's palm. The red light reflected off the smooth bronze of my arm. For a moment, nothing happened. After that, a wave of warmth flowed into my chilly limb. Red dots of light sparkled across my forearm. I sighed. The spell was working. Metal transformed back into flesh. I clenched and loosened my left fist, testing out the mobility.

"Much better," I said. "Thank you."

Rowan ran his hands up and down my arm. "You look fully healed. We should cast the gateway spell now."

All of a sudden, I realized that now was the perfect moment to talk about the baby. There was no one else around, for once. Besides, Rowan and I could certainly spare a few minutes before we began to cast our gateway spell.

"There's something I want to talk to you about first," I said.

Rowan's gaze turned intense. "Anything."

"We've agreed not to have a family and—" My words caught in my throat. *Why was this so hard?*

"It's all right," said Rowan. "I understand."

My heart lightened. Maybe Rowan guessed what was happening. That would make all of this a lot easier. "You do?" I asked.

"Sure," he replied. "Jicho is gone. That boy is like a son to both of us. It makes you think how nerve-wracking it would be to have a child of our own. Jicho is bad enough, right?"

"That isn't wrong." I swallowed past the knot of worry in my throat. "Here's the thing, though. You—"

At that moment, spots of white light pulsed from the vaulted ceiling. *Magick.* The bright points soon congealed into a loop of white energy that spun above our heads. My breath caught in my lungs. No question what that was.

"It's the round gateway," I whispered. "The one from Jicho's vision." I repeated the prophecy once more.

"Watch for the round gateway; it will bring you the lightning goddess and her consort. They must bring fire swords to the windings. Only then can you and Rowan kill Kronos."

Rowan scanned the loop of brightness as it whirled above our heads. "If that's a gateway, then I've never seen anything quite like it. We better pull in extra magick, just in case."

And with that, all chances of a baby conversation with my husband were now over. Not that this particular talk was headed in a great direction. We could return to it later. After all, there was a gateway opening before us now.

While keeping my gaze locked on the circular lights, I pulled fresh Necromancer energy into my body. Usually, I drew in power with my eyes closed since it was easier that way. But at this point, I wasn't taking any chances. Jicho said a lightning goddess and her consort would visit through a circular gateway. He didn't say that when they arrived, they'd be at all friendly.

Heavy silence filled the central feasting hall. The swirl of light by the ceiling flared more brightly, casting odd shadows onto the tapestries and floor. A charged sense of anticipation hung in the air.

My body quickly filled with so much Necromancer magick, I didn't even need to funnel the power to my left hand. The bones there began to glow on their own. Still, I kept my gaze locked on the circle of light above my head. A ring of perfect darkness filled its center. My mage awareness told me that whoever was coming though, it would be soon.

I shared a quick glance with Rowan. Every line of his rugged face was tight with determination.

Light pulsed in the center of the round gateway as a man and a woman tumbled through, landing on the floor in a crouch. Although their backs were facing us, I could still make out some basics about the pair. The woman was tall as me but far more curvy. Her long auburn hair cascaded down her back. The man beside her was broad shouldered and fit with short brown hair. Both of them were wore black body armor like none I'd ever seen before. It appeared not to be flexible. *Interesting.*

Something twitched behind the woman, and that's when I noticed it. She had a tail. It was long, black, and covered in some kind of scales. The end was as pointed as an arrow.

In our realm, we did have people with non-human body parts. They were called Changed Ones, and they were the unfortunate results of by brother Viktor's experiments in combining Casters with their animal familiars. My stomach sank. Was it possible that Viktor had somehow gotten to this woman and her realm?

The man lifted his right arm, and he was holding a severed head in his fist.

Wait, a head?

I rubbed my eyes, wondering if I was seeing things.

But once I lowered my hands, the man was still there, his back facing to us. And he still gripped a severed head in his hand. And what a head it was. The thing had the profile of a humanoid pig with green skin and a pair of large curlicue horns growing out of each temple. The man gripped the head by a single horn.

"The good news is, we killed the phase demon." The man tossed the head onto the floor before him.

"The bad news is, he phased us somewhere before he died," added the woman. Her tail perked up and tapped her shoulder. The woman looked to the arrowhead end. "What's up, boy?"

The tail gestured toward me and Rowan as if to say: *pay attention; there's something behind you.*

The woman slowly turned around. "Hello there," she said. If she was shocked to be in a strange place, she didn't show it.

The man turned around as well. He had mismatched eyes—one blue and one brown—as well as strong bone structure. The pair of us were a study in opposites. I was thin and dark haired, while the woman was curvy with long reddish locks. The man was pale and regal looking. At the same time, Rowan may be a king, but he always looked tanned and rugged.

The woman waved at us. "I said, hello there."

"Hello," I replied. "I'm Elea and this is Rowan. Who are you?"

"I'm Myla," said the woman.

The man gave us a chin-nod. "Lincoln."

"This may sound strange, but..." I debated how to ask the question, but decided quickly that there was no good way to pose this particular question. "Are you Changed Ones from an evil mage named Viktor?"

"That would be no," said Myla.

Rowan stepped forward. "Are you a lightning goddess, by any chance?"

"You could call me that," answered Myla. "Look, here's the situation. My husband Lincoln and I, we like to hunt demons for fun."

"Demons?" asked Rowan. "What are they? We don't have them in this world."

"So we're in a different world," said Lincoln calmly. "Good to know."

"To answer your question," continued Myla. "Demons are evil creatures who come from Hell."

Now I was confused. "What is Hell?" I asked.

Lincoln held up his hand. "Let me give it a try."

"Hasta la vista, muchacho," said Myla. She certainly had a strange way of speaking. Not unpleasant, just unusual.

"We're from different worlds," continued Lincoln. "In our world, there are sentient evil beings called demons."

"Understood," I said dryly. "In our world, there are sentient evil beings called *family*."

Myla grinned. "I like her."

Lincoln didn't all-out grin, but the edges of his mouth curled up slightly. "Glad we understand each other. So, Myla and I were hunting one of those demons, a one of a kind monster called a phase demon. It can open portals to other worlds. We killed the demon, but not before it sent us here. Now, we need a way to return home. Can you help us with that?"

Myla raised her pointer finger. "Just to add some context, I have a toddler at home who will get spoiled rotten if we aren't back by dinnertime." She glanced over to Lincoln. "You know your mother will feed Maxon nothing but ice cream and snickers bars until we show up."

Lincoln sighed. "Without a doubt."

My mouth fell open. Myla and Lincoln were not only married, but they also had a child together. On reflex, my hand went back to my belly.

I still hadn't told Rowan I was pregnant.

Myla tilted her head. "So, can you help us?"

"Yes," said Rowan. "Both Elea and I are mages. We

can open a magickal gateway that will return you to your home realm. But we ask for your help in return."

Lincoln narrowed his mismatched eyes. "What do you need?"

"I have a younger brother," began Rowan. "His name is Jicho. He was just stolen away by Kronos, an evil mechanical king. I suppose you might call Kronos a demon. Jicho is also a Seer, that's a mage who gets accurate visions of the future. Before he left, Jicho said that a lightning goddess and her consort would arrive through a circular gateway." Rowan gestured to Myla and Lincoln. "And here you are."

"Jicho's prophecy was very specific," I added. "We need your and your fire swords in order to defeat Kronos. Once that's done, we'll gladly take you home."

"It isn't a condition of our help," added Rowan. "Merely a request. We won't ask you to put your lives at risk without fully understanding what's at stake. Kronos is a fierce enemy who's backed by a mechanical army."

"Fierce, huh?" Excitement danced in Myla's eyes. Clearly the idea of fighting a new kind of demon was interesting to her. I'd judge her choice, but I was a woman who enjoyed covering the skeletons I conjured with pink gemstones.

"Very fierce," answered Rowan. "Elea and I are the

strongest mages in our realm, and Kronos had us defeated in minutes."

Myla pursed her kips. "Anything else we should know?"

"My parents," I replied. "They're the sentient evil beings that I spoke about before, so they are somehow involved with Kronos. It may be that they are working together, or they could all hate each other. It's a very confusing situation."

"I see." Lincoln bowed his head slightly. "Thank you both for being honest." He turned to Myla. "Well?"

With that, the two shared a long look. It was another of those stares that hid a silent conversation. With every passing second, the air in the chamber seemed grow thicker. Soon it was hard to pull in a single breath. After what felt like another eternity, the pair finally shared a slow smile.

Myla turned to me and Rowan. "Lincoln and I will help you."

Hope sparked in my heart. "Thank you."

"We have a little boy in our lives as well," said Lincoln. "If someone ever took my Maxon..." He shuddered. "I can't imagine your pain. We will certainly help you."

"Thank you," said Rowan. "Kronos said we had until tomorrow at midnight. If we didn't come to his dungeons by that point, he would kill Jicho." My husband slipped his hand into the folds of his jacket and pulled out a pocket watch. It was one that Amelia had designed for him, and it was a marvel of our realm. The piece even tracked day of the week and month. "According to my watch, we have about twenty hours."

"We need to rescue Jicho before that happens," I said. "So we can't waste any time. Rowan and I will cast a portal to take us to Kronos' realm of Quetum. Is there anything you need before you go?"

Myla shrugged. "I'm good."

Lincoln nodded. "Same here."

Rowan turned to me. "Ready to cast?"

My breath caught. We had less than one day to open a portal to Quetum, rescue Jicho and defeat Kronos... And let's not forget the part about my being pregnant and still needing to tell Rowan.

If it wasn't Jicho's life on the line, I'd say this was impossible. As it was, I'd say we won't give up, no matter what. So, I steeled my resolve, straightened my spine, and looked at Rowan straight on.

"Am I ready to cast?" I asked. "Absolutely."

And with that, the next stage of our adventure began. If only I could be sure it ended with all of us alive.

a minute later, Rowan and I had cast a gateway made of sparkling blocks of amethyst. Beneath that archway, a cityscape soon came into view.

Quetum.

It was a city was unlike anything I'd seen before. A grim charcoal sky loomed above. Piles of gray scrap metal stretched off in every direction. The place looked more like a trash heap than anything else. In the distance, a bronze clock tower cut up from the horizon line.

"That must be the Bezel Tower," I said.

Rowan's eyes narrowed as he took in the scene. "Definitely."

Before opening the gateway, Rowan and I had cast a seeing skull. The enchanted head told us Jicho was indeed being kept in the tower dungeons. It then confirm that it would be a terrible idea to cast a transport spell right into those very dungeons. Kronos had loaded the place with magickal traps. The skull suggested that we land in Quetum's labyrinth and look for a cat. We kept pressing with more questions, but the skull had no useful answers. In the end, we decided to open the gateway, ask for it to place us in the labyrinth and hope for the best. With a little luck, we would find a way to steal into the dungeons under the Bezel and rescue Jicho without Kronos being any the wiser.

Myla stepped up beside me. Angling her head, she scanned the cityscape through the gateway. "Looks like the archway opened up somewhere in the sky." She took a small step closer to the gateway's edge. "The ground doesn't look too far off, though. I think we can jump it."

I gulped. That might not look like a big jump for Myla, but I wasn't looking forward to it.

"We need to move quickly," said Rowan. "The longer we stand here, the more magick it takes from me and Elea."

"Got it," said Myla. Taking Lincoln's hand in hers, they leapt out the gateway in unison. I really wanted to do that as well, so I gave myself some internal words of encouragement.

You can bound out as well, Elea.

Just jump.

Go.

Any second now.

Leap.

More time passed.

I wasn't leaping.

Rowan stared at me with that intense gaze that I knew so well. He said two words. "Hold on." After that, he scooped me up into his arms and raced out the gateway.

I grabbed onto Rowan's neck with such force, I'm surprised I didn't snap a vertebrae or two. Pressing my forehead against my husband's shoulder, I didn't look up until I felt the thud of us landing on solid ground. Then I took a peek.

What I saw amazed me.

From the view of the gateway, it appeared as if the world of Quetum was totally flat. However, the four of seemed to have landed inside a long ravine of some kind. The walls around us were tall, metal and covered in bits of clocks. The floor was nothing but clock parts as well.

Definitely a labyrinth, just like the seeing skull said. Perfect.

Rowan set me on my feet. Leaning in , he spoke gently in my ear. "Are you all right?"

"I'm fine." Scanning the scene, I saw Lincoln and Myla were investigating the walls around us. "Everyone looks like they landed well, too."

"They did," replied Rowan. "We seem to have landed in the labyrinth."

"It's a decarinth," said a high-pitched female voice. "And you're going to die."

Now *that* was an ominous way to start a conversation.

Looking up, I saw that the speaker was none other than a bronze clockwork cat. *Another piece of the prediction from the seeing skull had come to pass*! She had large gear-shaped eyes, metal wire whiskers, and a segmented tail.

I tilted my head, thinking. It's true that on our world, announcing that someone's about to die less than friendly, but this was Quetum now. For all I knew, *you're going to die* is the kindest greeting they have. I decided to act that way and hope it was the truth.

"Hello," I replied. "I'm Elea. And you are?"

"Kitty. And this is Tank."

At the name Tank, a block of gears rose up beside her on gangly metal legs. It stood no higher than Kitty, which is to say, not more than a few feet tall. A pair of oversized eyes popped up from the top panel of the boxy creature. It waved its thin arms at us. I had a strange feeling of a power, as if the small creature were sending magick our way.

Magick? Inside a metal box creature? That couldn't be right.

I reached out with my mage senses, ready to check the power signature again. The feeling was nowhere to be found. I shook my head, deciding that it must have been a figment of my imagination. After all, I just stepped through a magickal gateway to another world. My mage senses might be all kinds of misaligned.

Speaking of the boxy creature, it stopped waving its arms. Kitty nodded at her square friend, and then turned to us once more.

"Tank says Hello," explained Kitty.

"Hello, Tank," I replied. "I'm Elea and this is Myla, Lincoln, and Rowan."

Myla's tail bobbed over her shoulder in a fast rhythm. She pointed at the arrowhead end. "And this is my tail. He hates being ignored."

"Hello, Myla's tail." Kitty started licking her front paw. It should have been a smooth feline movement, but with a clockwork cat, it became more stilted.

"So Kitty," said Myla. "I couldn't help but notice what you said before. Why do you think we're all going to die?"

Kitty didn't miss a beat of her licking. "You're in the Decarinth."

"Let me guess," said Rowan. "That's *deca* as in ten. *Rinth* as in labyrinth. Plus, these walls are all made up of different clocks counting down from ten to zero." Rowan looked to Kitty. "Why not twelve?"

Kitty sniffed. "Time is fluid here in Quetum."

"Is it now?" Rowan slipped his hand into the folds of his jacket and pulled out his pocket watch again. He frowned. "Ten hours have passed back in our home realm. We have twelve hours until Kronos's deadline." He looked to Kitty. "I don't suppose you can translate that into Quetum time?"

"Not possible," said Kitty. "Time works differently here, even from one hour to the next. Life works differently too, although that stays the same. I trust I make myself clear?"

"As mud," said Myla.

I stifled a smile. I was really starting to like her.

"We have no idea how long these twelve hours will really last," said Rowan. "So, we must work quickly." Stepping closer to the wall, he scanned a nearby watch face. "These clocks all read eight now."

Lincoln folded his arms over his chest and stared at Kitty. "What happens when the clocks all reach zero?"

Tank waved his little arms again. Kitty watched

silently, then turned back to us once more. "Something different every time, but it all ends the same. Whoever is in the maze, they all end up dead."

Kitty's final word echoed through my head.

Dead, dead, dead.

And this wasn't just me, there was my unborn child to think about as well.

The child I hadn't even told Rowan about yet.

Not to mention a dwindling countdown to save Jicho.

What a disaster.

"Now they read seven," said Rowan.

Spinning about, I scanned the clockwork walls myself. It wouldn't be easy to climb out of here, but I could cast some more skeletal servants to help. Closing my eyes, I searched my soul. The trip to Quetum had drained me. I had enough magick remaining for a spell or two, but nothing more. I need to pull in more energy.

Reaching out with my mage senses, I sought additional sources of Necromancer power. My consciousness spread out across many leagues. I found a few wisps of magick, but other than that, there was only empty and metallic space.

Certainly not enough Necromancer power to recharge me fully.

My chest tightened with worry. I rounded on

Rowan. "There's no Necromancer magick around. Can you pull in Caster magick?"

Rowan shook his head. "I already tried. I don't sense any here, but there's a residue in the air. If we had some months here, we could pull enough energy to recharge ourselves fully."

My stomach sank to my toes. Clearly, Rowan and I had to conserve our magick to fight Kronos. But in the meantime, we were all stuck in some kind of killer labyrinth? Not good.

Now Lincoln scanned the labyrinth walls. "They all read six," he announced.

I turned to Myla. "Can you summon your lightning? Cast some magick to get us out of here?"

"Sorry, Sweetie," Myla shook her head. "My powers are so I can move around souls in my world. I tried calling on them here when we got here. No go."

Kitty went back to licking her front paw. She and Tank were a little odd, but they didn't seem nefarious. Plus, the seeing skull said they could be helpful. Perhaps they'd to aid us, especially since our magickal options were looking limited.

Forcing a smile, I focused on the mechanical cat. "We need your help."

Kitty kept up her grooming. "Help with what?"

"Finding Kronos," I replied.

Kitty paused mid-lick. "And why do you wish to see our king?"

"Well, uh…" I looked to Rowan. My husband was excellent at saying a lot without telling people anything, mostly thanks to his years of spy work. "How would *you* explain our mission here?"

"We're here to kill Kronos," said Rowan. "Slowly, if possible." His voice lowered to a rumble. "That bastard took my brother."

Then again, Rowan blurt out everything in fifteen words or less.

Tank waved his arms around in a different rhythm, far more excited this time. Lowering her paw, Kitty watched him silently. Every nerve in my body went on alert. At last, the mechanical cat turned back to us. "We hate Kronos as well. We'll help you hunt him down."

Myla raised her pointer finger. "Define *we*."

"The Springlets," said Kitty. "That's me, Tank, and all the others. Quetum was our planet before Kronos made his Oculus Warriors. *That's* why we'll help you find Kronos."

Tank waved his tiny arms again. Once more Kitty translated. "Oh, and Tank says we'll help you kill him, too."

Lincoln raised his hand. "Down to five."

"Then we better move quickly." In a series of leaps,

Kitty scaled down the wall to join us at the bottom of the maze. My brows lifted. The edges on the walls were miniscule. Kitty may be a mechanical cat, but she certainly moved like the real thing.

"Kronos rules from the Bezel Tower," announced Kitty. She started stalking along the floor, her joints clicking softly as she stepped along. "Our so called king rarely leaves his tower—and it's the only structure around with a dungeon—so that's definitely where your Jicho is being held."

"We may have gotten some magickal advice along those lines as well," I said. It was good that Kitty's advice aligned with the seer skull I cast before. It meant it was more likely that we coud trust her and Tank.

"Now," continued Kityy. "We could storm the tower's front gates, but that's suicide. Besides, there are hidden back paths to enter the tower. Old refuse tunnels, mostly." She prodded at a particular spot with her paw. "And all of those tunnels empty out into this here Decarinth."

"Excellent," I exhaled.

Things were looking up.

Kitty poked at another spot on the floor with her paw. "Possibly. Kronos knows the Decarinth holds all the sneaky back ways into his precious Bezel Tower, so he changed the Decarinth. It kills off all life in the maze at the count of ten."

"That sucks," said Myla flatly.

"Four," said Lincoln.

My heart beat harder against my rib cage. I knelt down beside Kitty. "Anything we can do to help you find this entrance to the tunnels?"

Kitty stalked along a few more steps before speaking. "Can any of you cast any magick?"

"Elea and I are mages," said Rowan. "But we're low on power. We'd like to save it for Kronos."

"In that case," said Kitty. "The best thing you can do is be patient."

Atop the wall, Tank leapt up and town, waving his thin arms around once more. Kitty looked up and watched him for a moment. "You're no help to me here, Tank. Get the other Springlets and have them prepare to storm the front gate to the Bezel tower." She shot me a sly look. "We'll need a distraction if we're going to get access to Kronos."

Tank scaled the wall once more before disappearing over the top edge of the maze. For a moment when Tank was near, I felt that sensation again: the pull of magick. Once more, the feeling was gone before I could place it accurately. Besides, what was important right now was not that Tank may have some magickal residue.

It was getting out of the decarinth alive.

I focused my attention on Kitty. "You sent Tank away?"

"Yes," she meowed.

"But you just told us," I continued. "Anyone storming the front gate would be killed."

Kitty looked at me, tilting her head in a mechanical click. "That's right. Killed and turned into spare parts to make a new Oculus Warrior."

"But you can't do that." I stepped closer to Kitty. "Why would you all risk your life for us?"

Kitty's mechanical tail flicked behind her in a stuttering rhythm. "Because dying to us means different things than it does to you."

"Death is death," I said. "I don't understand."

"Really now?" asked Kitty. "How can you say that when nothing is the same to you as it is to others? The same is true of Springlets."

A chill crawled up my neck. "What do you mean?"

Kitty grinned, showing off a mouth full of sharp metal teeth. "I've met your parents, Elea of Braddock. They said you'd be arriving in Quetum in order to kill Kronos and rescue your Jicho."

All the breath left my body. "You know my parents?"

Kitty nodded. "They are freedom fighters. Why do you think Tank and I were waiting for you? Your parents have eyes and ears in the Bezel Tower. They heard you were coming. We have Springlets all over Quetum on the lookout for you."

Lincoln stared solemnly at Kitty. I could almost picture the plans and facts whirring through his brain. "So how did you get so lucky? You chose the exact spot where we landed."

"That was all Tank. He knows things. For example, Tank knows that there won't be any Oculus Warriors patrolling this area for another ten minutes." Lowering into a crouch, Kitty let out a mechanical hiss. "Now quiet down, all of you. The clocks are down to two. I need to concentrate." Her next words sent pangs of worry through me. "Time is running out."

All the clocks were marked with numerals from ten to zero. A single hand on their faces marked the count-down. With a soft tick, all the clock hands now switched to one.

Time was running out, indeed.

7

I couldn't believe it. All the clocks in the decarinth were now pointing to the numeral *one*. Once they all went to zero, that was it. Some exotic form of death awaited us, according to Kitty.

Speaking of Kitty, she kept sauntering down the decarinth, tapping her metal claws onto various watch faces.

Click, click, click.

I bit my lips together to stop my self from screaming.

Kitty paused before the right-hand decarinth wall. Tilting her head, she eyed a huge glass watch face set into the panel. Once again, she tapped the round surface with her claws.

Click, click, click.

Shaking her head, Kitty approached the next clock

face on the wall. This one was smaller than the last, but still fairly large compared to most. Kitty slammed her claws against the glass covering.

CLANG.

While all her other taps were muted sounds, this one echoed. A weight I didn't know I'd been carrying seemed to slip from my shoulders. There was no doubt about it: some kind of empty space waited behind that watch face. I popped my hands over my mouth to stop myself from cheering. Tank had said the Oculus Warriors patrolled this area. I didn't want to call any unnecessary attention.

"And here's a passageway," purred Kitty. She looked over her shoulder at the four of us. "I'll need some help to open this."

"I'm on it." Myla raced over. Moving with supernatural speed, she jammed the arrowhead end of her tail jammed into the edge of the watch face. With a snap, the face flicked out an inch. Myla then crammed her fingers into the opening and yanked the clock face off to one side. "I don't know how long that will hold open. It looks like it's set to snap back in place."

Stepping closer, I peered over Myla's shoulder. Sure enough, a tunnel opened up into the wall. The clock face itself stood about three feet high, and the passage appeared to be that tall as well.

Kitty hopped into the tunnel's mouth. Her gear eyes lit up in the darkness as she scanned the interior. "On second thought, maybe we should find another passageway."

"What's wrong?" I asked.

Kitty mewled. "This one will lead out to—"

At that moment, alarms of every kind began to buzz, ring, or wail. A thousand watch faces vibrated along the walls and floor of the decarinth. My heart sank. The clocks had reached the same time.

Zero.

The maze floor rumbled. I sucked in a shaky breath. Something was coming nearer. Kitty stood at the tunnel entrance and hissed. "This won't do. We must find another passage."

"That's fascinating," said Myla. "Now get into the tunnel already."

"No!" cried Kitty,

Suddenly, a clock gear as tall as Rowan came rolling down the center of the maze. It was like some kind of insane wagon wheel, only one with razor-sharp edges. I pictured the small round saw blades that had been attached to the Oculus Warrior's antennae. These looked just as deadly, only at a far greater scale. The gear rumbled past us. Everyone flattened themselves against the nearest wall.

We'd survived so far, but the rumbling under our feet grew more fierce.

More deadly gears were coming.

"Well?" Myla glared at Kitty.

"On second thought," said Kitty. "I think this tunnel is perfect." She turned about and scampered off into the darkness.

The rumbling grew stronger. This time, a mechanical whir filled the air as well. A second later, two more deadly gears rolled by. This time, the gears were concentrated by the right-hand wall. We all flattened ourselves by the left wall, which was farther away from our escape route.

"Come on," cried Rowan after the gears passed. "Everyone move. Now!"

The next few seconds were a flurry of moving bodies and a cramped passageway.

Myla slipped into the tunnel.

Then Lincoln.

The floor vibrated with more force than ever before. The mechanical whir became deafening. I looked to Rowan, ready to tell him to go in next.

"Don't even think about it." Rowan gripped my waist and hoisted me into the passage. Out of the corner of my eye, I saw a glint of metal as a dozen deadly gears spun toward us.

Once I got inside the tunnel, I found that it was about two feet deep before it opened up into a large corridor. The moment my feet hit the floor, I spun around, grabbed Rowan's wrists and hauled him inside. He yelled as I pulled him in.

Once Rowan was in my arms again, I began to pat down his body, just like he'd done to me after he healed my arm. In all truth, I may have been a little more frantic about the whole business than he'd been.

"Are you all right?" I asked breathlessly.

"I lost a shoelace," said Rowan dryly. "That's it."

Leaping up, I wrapped my arms around his neck and hugged him with everything I had inside me. "I never want to be scared like that again."

"That makes two of us," Rowan said with a low chuckle.

Outside, the clock face let out a series of low hisses before snapping back into place. A heartbeat later, we were all encased in perfect darkness.

Kitty hissed. "I can't see in the dark. I'm not that kind of cat! Now, what do we do?"

Jicho's prophecy echoed in my mind. *Fire swords.* "Don't worry, Kitty. I think Myla and Lincoln can help."

"We can?" asked Myla. "Oh, that's right. We totally can. I just got so caught up with the killer saw blade festival, I forgot both Lincoln and I have our baculum."

"Baculum?" asked Rowan.

"Short metal rods that Myla and I can ignite into any kind of weapon made from angelfire." As Lincoln spoke the words, a torch of white flame appeared in his hand. He pointed to the two silver rods at the base. "This is the baculum. They don't always have to be a sword." He shot a sly smile at Myla. "Amazing how many times we're scurrying around in the darkness, using these as torches."

Myla rolled her eyes. "Someone should write a book." After that, her own torch ignited in her hands. She looked around the passageway. "Here, Kitty, Kitty."

The cat leapt in front of Myla and hissed. "I hate that joke." She sniffed. "Now follow me." She sauntered off a few yards ahead and paused. "What are you waiting for?"

I couldn't speak for everyone else, but I knew what was making me cautious. "You didn't seem too excited about this passageway before." I scanned the walls. Everything was made from rusted metal. "What's wrong with this tunnel?"

"Oh that," Kitty sighed. "This passage leads only to two destinations. First, you can tumble right into an incinerator."

"I'll pass," said Myla. I completely agreed with her sentiment.

"Second," said Kitty. "You can open an access door to a barracks for the Oculus Warriors."

An image appeared in my mind: a dozen antennae with mini-saw endings. Those Oculus Warriors hadn't even attacked and I was terrified of them. Those things were the stuff of nightmares.

Even so, I forced on my calmest face. "Then we're off to the barracks."

That may have been what I said, but as we all followed Kitty deeper into the tunnels, I started to wonder something.

Maybe we had a better chance of survival with the incinerator instead.

8

*H*ours passed and we were all still marching through those tunnels. It wasn't an easy journey, either. Every so often, the passageway would click and shimmy. That's when kitty would mewl and tell us which wall to flatten ourselves against. After that, the tunnel would split into two. We'd stay on whatever said Kitty said did not end in a fiery death. Myla commented that that the whole thing seemed a little unnecessary. Kitty explained that it was another one of Kronos's failsafe measures to keep people out of the Bezel Tower. I was starting to wonder what kind of person even thought up such twisted security. Choose the wrong split in the tunnel and you get dumped into an incinerator?

Kronos gave cruel an entirely new meaning.

After a while, we started to chat a little. I debated about sharing the whole pregnancy revelation with Rowan, but then decided against it. I didn't want him to learn about our baby in a darkened tunnel with strangers nearby.

Instead of having the baby conversation, we asked Kitty a ton of questions about the Bezel Tower. She and Kronos had been designed to keep the tower, which is why she knew so much about how to sneak in and out. The said the Bezel Wand was supposed to go straight into the floor on the Control Room, but Kronos had figured out a way to pry it out, carry it around, and wield its magick. After that revelation, Kitty stated that she was done answering questions. She added that she'd already broken her feline vows by being as helpful as she had already. I had a cat of my own back home, so I understood.

With Kitty being nonresponsive, I then asked Myla more about angels and demons, a topic that both Rowan and I found fascinating. Turns out, Myla is part demon and Lincoln is part angel. I couldn't believe that. In fact, the news made me pause in my steps.

"So you're part demon," I said.

"Yup," replied Myla.

"And your tail is demonic as well?"

"Sure is." In the flickering torchlight, I could see

Myla's tail waving at me, so I waved right back. I liked Myla's tail, too.

I cleared my throat and tried to sound casual. "So you and Lincoln have a son."

"His name's Maxon," answered Lincoln. Even in the darkness f the tunnel, there was no missing the smile in Lincoln's voice as he said his son's name.

"We didn't plan on having a kid right away," said Myla. "But it all worked out."

"So you *wanted* a child?" I asked.

"Why not?" asked Myla.

"Well…" I gestured at her tail.

"Oh, the demon thing. It's not that simple. I'm aligned to what we call deadly sins. In my case, that's lust and wrath. Those can be good things in the right situations." Her and Lincoln shared a small smile. "A bloodline is what you make of it."

On reflex, my gaze swung to Rowan. He stood outlined in the tunnel, fixing me with a penetrating stare that could melt rock to lava. Did he guess why I was so curious about demons and babies? Again, this wasn't a conversation I wanted to have among strangers. I panicked. Words began tumbling from my mouth with no prior examination from my brain.

"Not that I have any reason to be curious personally,"

I added quickly. "Just asking in general. I find blood… and such things…utterly fascinating."

Stop talking, Elea.

Rowan's haze stayed fixed on me. I felt like a bug on a pin.

"I have a question for you," said Kitty.

Thankful for the reprieve, I turned my back to Rowan and focused on Kitty. Besides, it was nice that she'd decided to talk to us again. "Of course, you can ask me anything."

Kitty swung her head around to face me. Her gear shaped eyes reflected the torchlight as she spoke. "What I wish to know is this. What do you think of *your* bloodline?"

Bloodline. The word echoed through me in strange ways. Fresh bands of exhaustion wrapped around my body. My legs turned watery.

In all truth, my bloodline was nothing but a legacy of evil.

Thankfully, there were no torches near me. Otherwise, everyone could have noticed how all the color had drained from my face. Kitty thought my parents were freedom fighters. Meanwhile, I knew them as two people who wanted to kill me.

"Bloodline?" I swallowed past the lump of disgust that had lodged in my throat. "I don't know what you mean."

"Your parents have promised us freedom." With a series of small clicks, Kitty tilted her head. "Do you think they'll keep their word? Kronos tore apart my people for spare parts to make his Oculus Warriors. Now, we Springlets plan to storm the gate and cause a diversion, just so you have better odds when you fight Kronos. Tell me honestly. Do you think our sacrifice will be worth it?"

The truth fell from me in a jumble. "Honestly, I can't speak for my parents, only myself. We've promised to kill Kronos, and we will do that."

Kitty let out a staccato hiss. "Fine." With that, she turned on her paws and scampered off into the darkness. My heart sank.

That wasn't the reaction I was looking for.

I opened my mouth, ready to start a discussion about what we should do next. Lincoln set his finger over his lips and mouthed the word *quiet*. We waited silently. The scent of grease filled the tunnel, followed by soft clicks and whirs.

The hairs on my arms stood on end. I'd heard those noises before.

Oculus Warriors.

We'd reached their barracks.

At this point, I realized that everyone was starting at me. My mouth was still open, ready to speak. I looked to

Rowan and whispered. "How much time do we have before midnight?"

With any luck, the strange time phenomenon at Quetum would start to work in our favor. Perhaps we had hours to kill. If nothing else, we could wait a little while and try to pull in some more magick. Just because the Oculus Warriors were here, it that didn't mean we had to rush into death.

Rowan stared at his pocket watch and squinted. "We've one hour left before the deadline."

Disappointment and fear pressed onto my shoulders, heavy as stones. "One hour," I said in a low voice. "That means there's no time to lose. What do you wall think? Should we go into the barracks?"

Lincoln nodded.

Myla smiled.

Rowan stared at the tunnel ahead as if the intensity of his gaze might force Jicho to materialize out of thin air. I took that to mean *yes,* so I began tiptoeing down the last leg of the tunnel. All three of my companions followed behind.

Oculus Warriors, here we come.

9

*R*owan and I stood at the end of the access tunnel. Myla and Lincoln waited behind us, holding their torches. Kitty was still nowhere to be found.

A rusted access door loomed before me.

I set my ear against the metal. On the other side, there sounded a familiar chorus of mechanical whirs and clicks.

Oculus Warriors.

Rowan rested his hand gently on my shoulder. "We need something to help us to see inside," he whispered. "Or get some intelligence on what's within."

I knew what Rowan what kind of *something* Rowan was talking about.

Magick.

"It's a risk," I said in a low voice. "We're both low on magick."

Rowan shrugged. "There are some novice spells that wouldn't be too taxing, especially if we used our hybrid power."

"True."

My thoughts then spun through every kind of spell we could cast. The choice was overwhelming. Over the past months, Rowan and I had practiced dozens of spell combinations. In each case, we took a Necromancer and Caster spell, brought them together, and made something more. There were castings for enemy insight, seeing through walls, mapping the placement of possible foes, the list went on and on.

And there were ones for seeing the future, but really, that was Jicho's area of expertise.

My poor Jicho.

Somewhere below this building, our precious boy was being held by Kronos. I could only hope Jicho was safe.

At that thought, the perfect spell appeared in my mind. "How about the bird's eye spell? It combines Necromancer spell crone hands with the Caster jila bird."

Rowan rubbed his chin slowly. "Crone hands increase the power of any spell. The jila bird gives insight on what will help you. It's perfect."

Rowan laced his fingers with mine. A trickle of warm Caster energy flowed from his hand into mine, while I sent necromancer power to him. A moment later, both our free palms glowed with faint violet light. Since this was a compound spell, I would speak my incantation first.

> *"The beauty of gnarled bone*
> *The strength that drives its touch*
> *Bring me the hand of a crone*
> *To heal, give, and clutch."*

Tendrils of purple mist lifted off my free palm. The small cloud quickly congealed into the form of a skeletal hand that hovered before me at shoulder height. Normally, I could use real bones in the nearby ground and repurpose them in my spell. However, on Quetum there was nothing around but metal for miles. Even so, my magick was strong enough to create the skeletal hand on its own. As the spell requested, the bones were gnarled, full of wisdom, and ideal. I focused on Rowan. "Your turn."

Rowan lifted his free hand. His palm still glowed with purple light. Closing his eyes, Rowan whispered his incantation.

"Color. Beauty. Sight. Fly to me, little bird."

Violet-colored mist lifted off Rowan's free hand, congealing into the shape of a small bird with a white body and a red and green tail. The bird fluttered over to land on the skeletal crone's hand. Once safely on its perch, the bird focused its tiny button eyes at Rowan, as if to ask: *What do you wish of me?*

"Take strength from the hand of the crone," said Rowan. "Then give your gifts to Elea's eyes." He set his hand on my shoulder, just so there would be no confusion about whose eyes we were talking about. Low level spells needed extra clarification like that.

The bird tweeted once and then pecked at the skeletal hand beneath it. The bones there glowed blue with power. The brightness moved up the bird's stick-like legs, across its rounded little belly, and settled onto its multicolored tail. Those feathers now gleamed with shades of red and green that were so strong, they lit up the entire hallway. For the first time, I could see every detail of the rusted walls and moldy floor.

Myla and Lincoln stepped closer. Lincoln was the first to speak. "Your magick is beyond beautiful."

"Thank you." I turned my attention to the little bird and clucked my tongue in its direction. "Come on, now. Finish our your work. Give me your gifts."

The jila bird pecked at the bones beneath it once more. The crone's hand had been hovering place for some time. Now, it rose up until the bird was at eye level with me. I closed my eyes and felt the soft tickle of feathers, followed by low chuckles from my companions. I couldn't see what was happening, but I could imagine it easily enough. The bird would have twisted around so its tail feathers were by my closed eyes, and then shaken itself so the feathers—and more importantly, the magic—brushed across me. A calming chill sunk into my eye sockets.

When I opened my eyes again, the bird and skeletal hand were gone. Rowan, Myla and Lincoln stepped back. They were all staring at me so intensely, I started to worry that the spell had gone wrong somehow.

I patted my eyes. "Is everything all right?" I asked.

"Yes," said Rowan, his voice husky. "The whites of your eyes are glowing either red or green. It's lovely. Do you have any insights yet? Dangerous things will seem to have a red light in them that only you can see. The same is true for green. That means it will help you."

I scanned the far wall. "I don't see anything different." I carefully looked over Myla, Lincoln and Rowan as well. "None of you look lit up in any way, either."

"What about behind you?" asked Rowan.

"Good idea." I shook my head. "Of course." I turned around gasped. "The entire door glows with red light. Do you see that as well?"

"No," said Rowan. "The spell is working. The casting will be at its most powerful now. For a little while, you'll be able to see through things as well. Can you see anything from the other side of the wall?"

Every nerve in my body went on alert. Because I did see something on the other side of the wall. It was a vision in red light that shown through the metal door.

An Oculus Warrior.

The monster was only a few inches away from me, and it was pushing on the other side of the door. All thought vanished from my head. The Oculus Warrior gave one last shove against the side of the door and it spun around like a top.

One moment, I was standing in the passageway with Rowan, Myla and Lincoln. The next it was just me and a hundred Oculus Warriors standing in neat rows by the low metal benches they must use as beds. None of them seemed to notice me, so I stood perfectly still.

The barracks themselves were long, rectangular, and made entirely of bronze. I was standing on one short end of the rectangle. The exit door was at the other side because, well, that just seemed to be how my day was going now.

The only good thing? The other Oculus Warriors kept facing toward the opposite wall and the exit door.

I balled my hands into anxious fists. Every nerve in my body was urging me to run, but right now? No one was attacking me with evil metal antennae, so I was going to stay put. If anything, the Oculus Warrior beside me seemed more curious than combative.

My heart beat so hard, I could feel my pulse in my throat. I scoured my mind for some way out of this disaster.

Think, Elea. There must be a way to escape.

The Oculus Warrior who'd pushed the door stepped up closer to me. Up close, these things looked like a mish-mash of random parts and smelled of old grease. The warrior poked my shoulder. I didn't move.

I scanned the warrior from head to toe. It didn't have any red or green glow to it. Neither did the other warriors in the room. If they were a danger to me, they'd be giving off red light, right? At least, that's what has happened with the spin door.

Behind me, I could hear faint scratches and thuds against the access door. From this side, the thing didn't even look much like a door at all. It blended in perfectly with the other metal wall panels that lined the room. Sweat beaded along my temple.

Please, let me get out of here alive.

The Oculus Warrior leaned in closer and inhaled deeply. What was it doing now? Sniffing? My day was growing stranger by the moment.

After that, the warrior stood up straight again. Red light encased it entirely. The spell was warning me.

Oh, no.

A low croak of a voice came out from under the warrior's helmet. "Kitty." Based on the tone the warrior used, I'm guessing it was not a friend of our clockwork cat. And evidently, I smelled like her.

One by one, every one of the Oculus Warriors took on the same red glow, at least to my eyes. It was the spell warning me that danger was arising.

I was starting to think this wasn't the most useful spell. It's not like I needed to have the illusion of these monsters glowing with red light to know they were dangerous. Moving in unison, all the warriors turned around to face me. As they moved, their boots hit the floor in a perfectly synchronized pair of stomps.

"Attack!" cried the warrior closest to me.

My mind soaked in every aspect of this moment. The pounding behind me became more fierce as Rowan tried to reach me. Hundreds of Oculus Warriors spouted identical antennae from their backs. Some of the metal arms ended with round saws. Others held knives or corkscrews. Still more had needles.

And then, I saw it.

All their helms glowed with the faintest green light. That had to be a good sign. At last, my mind broke out of its haze of fear. I sorted through everything that had happened since we met Kronos. How Kitty said that the mechanical king had torn apart her friends to make his Oculus Warriors…The power held in Kronos's walking stick…And the green hue that emanated from those identical helms over mismatched bodies.

Suddenly, I knew exactly what to do. Cast skeletal sledges. As many as I could. These were like skeletal servants, only far more hefty and battle hardened.

In other words, they were perfect for my plans.

Pulling in magick from the corners of my soul, I spoke the incantation.

"Power from bone
Blood and stone

Warriors of might
Battle and fright"

This time, I wouldn't be able to share my powers with Rowan, so the spell would use only Necromancer energy. The bones in my left hand glowed blue.

And that's when the Oculus Warrior closest to me struck. Its back antennae popped out and, lucky me, those thin arms ended with spinning saw blades. One sliced into my right shoulder. Pain radiated down my arm. With all my will, I pushed out the magick from my uninjured arm and out into the world.

Blue mist filled the room. When the cloud dissolved, a dozen hefty skeletons stood around me in a semi circle. "My sledges," I called. "Tear off their helms."

I didn't wait to see what the sledges did. Reaching over, I gripped the edge of the hem of the Oculus Warrior nearest to me. Wrapping my fingers around the bottom lip of the massive helm, I pulled with all the strength in my good arm. The Oculus Warrior counter attacked, jamming round saw blades into my thigh and back.

I heaved harder. Warm blood dripped down my arm and pooled at the base of my spine. At last, the helm gave way. I tore it from the Oculus Warrior's head. The metal monster stood in place for a moment.

After that, it collapsed into a pile of spare parts. Gears, wire, and springs littered the floor. Around me, my skeletal sledges were doing the same thing. They pulled off helm after helm, turning more of the Oculus Warriors into junk piles. Kronos had used the helms to transform the remains of Springlets into Oculus Warriors. Taking away the helm returned them to their previous state.

More blood dripped onto the floor. My head felt too light on my shoulders. Nearby, my skeletal sledges were still fighting the remaining Oculus Warriors, but there was something else I needed to do. I squinted, trying to focus my addled mind.

Door. That's it. I needed to get Rowan.

With hesitant steps, I turned to face the wall behind me. I pushed on the panel, leaving streaks of red blood everywhere I touched. White spots appeared in my vision. I wouldn't stay awake for much longer. A thin cord glowed between one of the seams between the metal wall panels. I smiled. The wire was shining with green light.

I gripped the edge of the cord and pulled. The force of the effort sent me falling onto my knees, but the move worked. The door swung halfway open. Myla, Lincoln, and Rowan rushed inside. My husband pulled me against him.

"You're going to be fine, Elea." He began whispering the words to a Caster incantation for healing. The last thing I remembered was the warm touch of his hands on my wounds. After that, everything became quiet and dark.

10

I awoke with a gasp. Rowan held me in his lap, his solid arms encircling me with warmth and love. His lips brushed the shell of my ear. "You're healed," he said in a low voice. "The Oculus Warriors are all gone. We're safe here for a few minutes."

I blinked a few times to clear my head. Where was I? What was happening? The memories appeared in a flash. I'd been fighting Oculus Warriors. One had sliced into me with the round blades. My eyes widened. I'd lost a lot of blood. I may have recovered, but I wasn't the only one to worry about.

"I'm fine," I rasped. "But what about the…" I couldn't force the word from my mouth.

"Baby?" finished Rowan.

"Yes." My heart cracked. *This wasn't how I'd planned to have this conversation.* "The baby."

"The baby is fine." Rowan fixed me with an unreadable stare. "You're fine."

After so much panic and worry about the whole topic of pregnancy, words began pouring out of me in a rush. "I'd been trying to tell you, but I didn't know how. It wasn't my plan for you to find out this way. I didn't want to shock you."

"It wasn't a shock." Rowan cupped my face in his hands, guiding our gazes together. "I suspected something back in the tunnel. You were asking Myla so many questions about her son; I could tell children were on your mind. Then, you kept resting your hand on your belly. So I had a good sense what was happening. And then when I healed you, my magick sensed the child."

"And your magick says that the baby is fine." For whatever reason, I needed to hear that last part again. "Right?"

"Yes, she's fine."

My pulse stuttered. "*She?*"

"That's right. A girl." Rowan let out a long breath. "I know we never planned to have children, and for very good reasons. But now? I keep picturing a little girl with your long dark hair and wise brown eyes." Leaning in, he ran the length of his nose along mine. "The more I think about it, the more I'm comfortable with the idea. I just want you to know that."

Words began tumbling from me again. "But you just almost lost me to evil mechanical monsters. That might be clouding your thoughts."

"No matter what happens," said Rowan. "Know this. I love you with all that I am." I met his gaze again. Nothing but true respect and love shone in Rowan's green eyes. "Everything else, we'll work it out. Together."

There were a thousand things I could say to him now. I wanted to share how the last year with him had been the best of my life. How much I loved waking up at his side. And how he was my true partner in both joy and trouble. Only two words fell from my lips, though. "That's good."

Something tapped at my heel. Looking down, I saw Kitty perched by my feet. Her large gear eyes stared up at me. "You better be worth this."

I blinked hard. *Kitty was here? That didn't seem real.* "You ran off."

"To let Tank know to prepare the charge," said Kitty. "We're still invading the entrance bridge to the tower. Tank is waiting for us to get him. We can't attack without getting Tank first."

"You could have mentioned that fact," I said. "We thought you'd deserted us."

Kitty lifted her chin. "But I'm a feline." And that was the sum of her explanation.

Again, since I'd had cats of my own, I knew exactly what Kitty meant here. Felines do what they want, how they want, and when they want.

Kitty sniffed. "Also, I went and checked on your Jicho. Bronze boy? Bald head?"

My heart thudded against my rib cage. "That's right."

"He's alive," said Kitty. "Kronos had him locked up in a magickal prison cell. The false king is even waiting down in the dunegons with him."

Jolts of both excitement and dread moved through me. "I don't like the idea of Kronos down there with Jicho, but if that's the case, where's that Bezel Wand of his?"

"He keeps the want in the control tower room," says Kitty. "Unless he's smiting someone with it, Kronos allows it to eke out a little power to keep the rest of the planet going. Barely."

Myla stepped closer. "The Bezel Wand?" she asked. "You mean that walking stick thingy that's jam packed with extra vitamins and magickal power?"

Rowan nodded. "We just need to sneak in there and get it."

I looked to Kitty. "What do you think? Is it possible to steal it?"

"Kronos is known for leaving the Bezel Wand unguarded," said Kitty. "Sometimes people from other worlds come to visit us." She lowered her voice. "I think they come to steal the Bezel Wand, but they never do. Everyone says the Oculus Warriors get them first." She shivered. "All of them end up dead."

Her words set my thoughts racing. "But what about my parents?" I asked. "When they came here, did they try to steal the Bezel Wand?" *Because that's something I'd totally expect them to do.*

Kitty lifted her chin. "They didn't touch it. They're freedom fighters who have no interest in magick or gateways."

I frowned. "That really doesn't sound like my parents."

Myla tapped my shoulder. "Hey, muchacha. I'm getting worried on the timeline here."

I looked her over intently. "I'm not sure what you said, but I think it's something like, we're running low on time."

"It was," said Lincoln. That smile sound was back in his voice.

"I'll take Myla and Lincoln to the Windings," said Kitty. "That's where Tank is hiding."

I'd been leaning against Rowan's chest before. Now I sat bolt upright. "Did you say windings?" I asked.

Kitty sniffed. "Of course, that's what I said. The Windings. Capital W. It's a little town. Was a little town. Then Kronos razed it. Now the place is a gully and Tank is hiding out in there. He's very important so we have to get him before we invade anything."

I snapped my fingers, trying to force a memory. "Jicho said something about the Windings before. He said the lightning goddess and her consort were to go there with their fire swords. It must mean that Myla, Lincoln, and Kitty should all go get Tank together."

Rowan frowned. "So you and I face down Kronos alone." Based on the angry edge to his voice, I could tell my husband wasn't enamored with this idea.

Myla raised her hand. "Full disclosure. I couldn't help overhearing about the pregnancy thing." Her tail popped up over her shoulder, the arrowhead end moving in an up-and-down, nodding motion. She gave it a wry glance. "We know you heard it too, boy. Anyway, I was a nightmare when I was pregnant. I'm not a fan of Elea facing some mechanical king without extra backup. I don't care what this random prophecy says."

Kitty turned toward Myla and Hissed. "What about

the Springlets? We're about to commit mass suicide against Oculus Warriors, and all just to provide a diversion so Kronos won't return to the control room. Don't we deserve some help?"

"Okay," sighed Myla. "The cat has a point. What are the Spinglets going to do against Oculus Warriors, exactly? Cute them to death?"

How very true.

I forced myself to stand. I had something to say, and it was the kind of statement best made while on your own two feet. "The Spinglets do deserve our support," I declared. "Besides, Jicho's prophecies are never wrong. If Myla and Lincoln are supposed to go to the Windings with their fire swords, than that should be the plan."

Myla smacked her lips. "Even so, I'm still not a fan of prophecies. People who have visions cause no end of trouble."

Lincoln stepped up to her side and spoke in a sly voice. "But those visionaries are often right, are they not?" The way he asked the question, I got the feeling this wasn't the first time Lincoln and Myla had encountered a vision of some kind.

"Yes, they often are." Myla tapped her cheek while her tail swished back and forth. "How about this? We go to this Windings place, get Tank, raid the bridge, slice down all the Oculus Warriors with our baculum, and then come back and check on Elea? Hopefully she and Rowan have this Bezel Wand and everything will be fine. But, you know, just in case."

Rowan stood beside me. "I like that idea very much."

Kitty mewed happily. "Good. We have a plan. I'll show Elea and Rowan the secret back stair to the control room. You two sneak inside and get the Bezel Wand. Lincoln, Myla and I will go to Windings."

I looked to Rowan. "Do you have any magick left?"

"A small amount. How about you? Any remnants of the bird's eye spell left?"

I quickly scanned the room. "Nothing looks lit up with red or green light. That doesn't mean the spell is over, though. I may have a little more use out of it." Closing my eyes, I searched my soul for additional reserves of power. Very little remained. I even reached out to the nearby landscape to seek out more Necromancer energy. There was none to be found. "So you know, I don't have much more in the way of stored magick. Conjuring the skeletal sledges took a ton out of me."

"It's the same with me. I might have gone a little overboard with healing spells." He gave me a wry smile. "Still, I have enough in me for one more. We'll need to save it for good use."

"Agreed," I said. "How much time do we have left before Kronos's deadline?"

Rowan pulled out his pocket watch. "Ten minutes."

My eyes widened. "In that case, we better get moving." I turned to Kitty. "Where is this secret passage of yours?"

Kitty pranced over to a nearby wall and tapped on the metal. One of the bronze panels instantly swung open. "Go to the top of the stairs. The access panel there goes right to the control room. And later, if you like, you can take the downward direction for the dungeons. I'm off to get Tank."

I narrowed my eyes at Kitty. Sure, she had been house cat for the Bezel Tower, which explained why she knew her way around so well. Still, her main point of concern always seemed to center on Tank. Something about all that didn't add up.

"Why do you need Tank before you can start the attack?" I asked.

"I'm a cat and I'll never tell." She looked at me coyly over her shoulder. "At least, not until I'm ready."

In other words, there was a story here and it would have to wait.

First, Rowan and I had some stairs to climb and a Bezel Wand to steal.

And only minutes to do so before Kronos's terrible deadline was up.

I stepped into the passageway and started taking the stairs at a run.

owan and I raced up the spiral staircase. Like the access tunnels leading out from the decarinth, this space was made entirely out of metal. We soon reached the top. The faint outline of an access panel loomed before us. A thin cord beside it glowed with the palest shade of green.

I grinned. The bird's eye spell was still working, at least a little. It was showing me the cord I needed to pull in order to enter the control room.

With trembling hands, I gripped the cord and tugged. The panel swung open without a sound. Bands of anxiety tightened around my throat. After so much worry and all our journeying, we were finally here: the control room.

Now, all we needed to do was grab the Bezel Wand

and we'd have all the magick needed to rescue Jicho. Rowan and I shared a long look and silent nod.

This was it.

We were going in.

Rowan entered the control room first. I tiptoed in behind him. The space was a great round chamber. Half of the room was covered in tall bronze panels. For some reason, they made me think of a line of towering ovens.

Not a comforting thought.

The other side of the circular room was a single round window that overlooked Quetum. The official entrance and exits—a pair of hefty bronze doors—flanked either side of the curved window pane. I stepped closer to inspect the view. I hadn't seen Quetum since we first opened the gateway here. It struck me again how gray and gloomy the skies were. The landscape was a dingy sheet of metal and trash that stretched out for many leagues. A foul taste filled my mouth. At one time, the must have been a lovely place.

Kronos did this.

He ruined this planet.

Forcing myself away from the window, I scanned the control room floor. It was made of concentric bronze rings that converged in the middle of the room. At that central point, the Bezel Wand stuck up waist-high from the floor. Back in the tunnels, Kitty told us how Kronos hindered the central engine that powered the planet by pulling the Bezel Wand from its proper spot. The way the control room was built, the wand should fit fully into the floor. Instead, the base of the wand was lightly embedded in the surface. The barest of glows lit up the moonstone top. As a mage, I knew what that meant. The wand was either low on power, or it was installed so that it only gave enough power to keep the planet from dying entirely.

I didn't think I could hate Kronos more, but as of this moment, I did.

Rowan and I scanned the space carefully. As Kitty had predicted, the room was empty. We approached the Bezel Wand. My heart rate sped. Jicho was almost as good as rescued. I reached toward the wand. Excitement lightened my soul.

Rowan grabbed my wrist, stopping me.

"I don't like this," he said in a low voice. "It's too easy." He glared at the Bezel Wand as if it would explode. "We should take the stairs to the dungeon. Save Jicho that way. This wand sets off my mage senses."

"Really? I didn't feel anything." I reached for the Bezel Wand once more. My fingertips almost brushed the device when the sensation hit me. Numbness crept into my hand. My skin on my arm felt so itchy, I wanted to scream. This was just like what happened when Kronos's spiders bit me.

I pulled my hand back like it had been on fire. "I sense it, too."

"What kind of magick is it? A protection spell of some kind?"

"I don't know, but I do remember what Kitty said before. People come in here to steal the Bezel Wand, but none leave alive." I hugged my elbows. "We have time left. Let's go to the dungeons."

A series of clangs sounded behind us. Turning around, I saw the bronze panels lining the wall were now hitting the floor. Before, those panels had reminded me of a line of tall ovens. Now it struck me that those many oven doors were falling open to reveal a large space hidden behind them.

In the center of that room stood none other than Kronos.

Pure rage heated my bloodstream. Kronos had been watching us this entire time. What did that foul monster want?

A line of Oculus Warriors waited behind the mechanical king. Jicho waited silently at Kronos's side. My sweet boy still appeared to be made of bronze. His beloved face was streaked with metallic-colored tears. His wrists were still tied. More cords had been wrapped around his head and mouth, preventing him from speaking.

My heart lurched at the sight. On reflex, I ran for Jicho, my only thought to hold him in my arms and offer comfort. I took a half-step, but stopped myself before going further. This wasn't a time for rash action. Rowan and I needed to stop and plan. Kitty and the Springlets were about attack the main gate with Myla and Lincoln. Once that was done, Myla and Lincoln had promised to return. With their help and the element of surprise, we might be able to save Jicho yet.

Kronos adjusted his round mirror glasses. "I'm so disappointed. You were supposed to touch the Bezel Wand. Most of my prey does right away, you know."

My eyes widened as I fully realized the truth. "My parents didn't get sent into exile here."

Kronos sniffed. "Exile? No. I lured them here." He gestured around the room. "If you cast a spell in search of potent magick to steal, then your casting will always lead you to this very spot. Your parents wanted to break out of exile and return to your realm. So they needed more magick to even try that, didn't they?"

I didn't answer. The fact that my parents would try to steal magick seemed very plausible to me. In fact, it was the first thing I thought of when Jicho came to me with his vision. I assumed my parents were not only returning, but with an army.

"No need to speak, I can see you agree." Kronos grinned, showing his mouth of sharp bronze teeth. "In general, I find that people who have magick always want more of it, no matter how much they have. So I lure them here and take that nasty power off their hands. This control room...the way I set up the Bezel Wand...it's all a trap. When you grip the Bezel Wand, it pulls out all your magick, if you have any to give. Your parents almost fell for it, but then they stopped, just as you did. After that, they did the strangest thing. They went into hiding. I'd heard of them and their power. I simply had to drive them out into the open again."

A chill crawled up my neck. "This is all a trap for my parents."

"So true. Don't get me wrong. You would have been a nice appetizer of magick, but I'm waiting for the main course. I want your parents to come out of hiding." Kronos gave me a sly smile. "Too bad about Kitty and your other friends."

My blood ran cold. "What do you mean?"

"There's no real attack on the main gate. Not any more." An evil edge crept into Kronos's voice. "They're all dying or dead."

All of a sudden, it felt as if the floor was falling out from under me. "No, that can't be right."

Kronos shrugged. "Look out the window and see for yourself."

I hated giving this man my back, so I hesitated. Rowan set his hand on my shoulder, his touch reassuring. "Go take a look," said Rowan. "I'll keep an eye on him."

"Yes," chuckled Kronos. "He'll keep an eye on me."

With hesitant steps, I turned around and peered out the window. The Bezel Tower was surrounded by a moat of dark liquid. A single bridge connected the tower to the mainland, and that structure was covered in Oculus Warriors. They were slicing little Spinglet animals into spare parts. I popped my hand over my mouth. "You're a monster," I whispered.

"Thank you," said Kronos. "I must admit, Kitty had me fooled for a while, but then she made the massive error of leading you right into the barracks for my Oculus Warriors. After you fought them, you all were kind enough to speak every last plan in a loud and clear voice. It was all rather easy from there."

I stared in horror as below me, the Oculus Warriors tore through the tiny figures rushing across the bridge. I didn't see Kitty, Tank, Myla, or Lincoln in the fight. But there were so many little mechanical bodies on the bridge. Even more toppled into the dark waters. They were all probably gone, never to be seen again. Rage corkscrewed up my spine.

I rounded on Kronos. "How could you?" I asked. "You were created to protect this world and their people. Kitty was the house cat and you were created to protect the engine. But you didn't want to. You decided you'd steal the power for yourself."

Kronos pulled on the rope that tied him to Jicho, forcing the child closer. Fresh tears streamed down the boy's face. "Flesh mages like this one created our planet." Kronos leaned in closer to Jicho, snapping his teeth by the child's ear. Jicho whimpered. "I was designed by weak things such as you. My purpose was to build my webs and trap those who would destroy the engine of Quetum." Kronos lifted his finger and set it on Jicho's neck. "But then, I got a taste for it. Trapping. Blood."

Before, a bronze cord had whipped out from Kronos's finger to wrap around Jicho's wrists. Now, a fresh line of bronze extended from Kronos's hand. Moving whip fast, the cord wrapped around Jicho's neck and torso, winding the poor child up like a cocoon. Jicho fell to his knees, openly weeping. Hot tears rolled down my cheeks as well. What wouldn't I give to help Jicho right now?

"You were a springling," said Rowan, his voice low and hoarse. "Kitty was the cat and you were a spider."

"Was?" asked Kronos. "I still am."

Bronze light shimmered across the many cords that made up the mechanical king. With a series of snaps, Kronos's body expanded until he was no longer human in the least. Instead, Kronos had transformed into a giant metallic spider with eight massive legs. A wide face was now set directly into his huge body. The Spider-Kronos's round glasses became into a pair of large and bulbous eyes. Pincer teeth lined his long mouth. "See what I've become? I'm perfect. And so I also perfected the Springlets as well. I turned them into Oculus Warriors."

All the while, Jicho still kneeled at the spot where the Spider-Kronos had yanked him to the floor. The boy's hands and mouth still bound by bronze cords, as were his neck and torso. His shoulders heaved with silent sobs. Seeing that, a single thought consumed me.

I had to get Jicho out of here. There must be a way.

The Spider-Kronos crawled closer. "Now, here is what will happen. You, Elea of Braddock, will step over to the Bezel Wand and grasp it. Then your husband will do the same. All your magick shall drain into the device until you're dead. Once that happens, I will send the boy back to your home world.

Rowan pulled me against his side. "We refuse."

"You're lying again," I said. "You've no plans to release any of us."

"You're quite right," said the Sipder-Kronos. "I am hunting larger prey. Aren't I?" His long legs clacked on the metal floor as the Spider-Kronos angled himself to look into the opened panel where Rowan and I had first stepped into the room. There, framed on the threshold, stood my parents.

The Sire of Souls and the Lady of Creation.

They were here.

Many emotions churned though me at once. Disgust. Fear. And while I hated to admit it, I felt a little bit of joy, too.

The Sire stepped forward. Like always, he looked austere with his dark armor, pale skin, and strong bone structure. His brown eyes locked with mine. "Dear daughter," he said. "We didn't understand until we came to this planet...until we were the ones who were about to be drained of power for someone else's gain."

More tears filled my eyes. "Don't you dare speak to me."

The Lady stepped forward next. She looked tall and lithe in her emerald green gown. Her golden hair hung down her back in waves. "We felt the trap on the Bezel Wand, and we saw the devastation of the land. In that moment, your father and I realized what we had been doing was wrong. We'd fooled ourselves that we were transforming worlds to make them more beautiful and safe. But in reality, we'd only devastated the lovely plans that already existed, including the glorious gifts that were our own children." She looked to the Spider-Kronos. "It's in a spiders nature to cast webs and trap things. As intelligent creatures, we must control our baser urges."

The Spider-Kronos clacked his pincer-teeth together. "The family reunion is over. Now give over your power to the Bezel Wand and I'll spare your daughter."

"You don't understand, do you?" The Lady shook her head. "The Sire and I needed to change, and that meant a sacrifice." She stepped over to the Bezel Wand and gripped the moonstone that sat at its top. Nothing happened. "You see?" she asked. "We gave up our magick. The Sire and I are normal mortals now."

I couldn't believe what I was hearing. My parents were power mad. That was the essential truth of their existence. Yet, I couldn't deny what I saw with my own eyes. The Lady touched the moonstone and nothing happened. She had no power to steal anymore.

"What? No!" The Spider-Kronos's eight legs shifted in an agitated rhythm. "Don't you understand? It takes massive amounts of power to maintain myself and my Oculus Warriors. My Bezel Wand is almost empty. I NEED YOUR POWER! You must have given it to your husband." The Spider-Kronos rounded on the Sire. "You! Go to the wand! Hand over your magick."

My father crossed the room and set his hand atop the wand. Again, nothing happened. "My wife speaks the truth. We needed to atone for what we'd done. We made a sacrifice. Giving up magic—and staying here to help the Springlets—that was our way to try to make amends."

I looked to Rowan. The question lingered in my gaze, unspoken but still there. *Is this real?*

Rowan nodded slowly. *It is real. They gave up their power.*

"If you don't have magick, then you're useless to me," snarled the Spider-Kronos. "Oculus Captain! Prepare!"

Behind the throne, I noticed how one warrior stood slightly taller than the others: the Oculus Captain. With a series of clicks, all its back antennae deployed, surrounding it in a halo of thin metal arms that ended with the same weapon.

This Oculus Captain carried throwing daggers.

The Spider-Kronos rounded on me. "You didn't think I'd allow hand to hand combat, did you? Not when you know the secret of my warrior's helms."

On reflex, I set my hand on my throat. This couldn't be happening. I wasn't standing here to watch my parents die. The two of them stood side by side, awaiting their end with dignity.

"Oculus Captain!" cried the Spider-Kronos. "Attack!"

Daggers flew across the room, landing with precision into the torsos of my parents. Blood bloomed across my mother's chest. Red droplets fell from my father's fingertips. They both slumped to the floor, side by side.

I fell onto my knees. Every muscle in my body quivered with grief. Rowan knelt beside me. Like he had so many times before, my husband whispered in my ear.

Only this time, the words were ones I didn't expect.

"Look at the back doorway," whispered my husband. "The one we came through." Then, Rowan spoke in a louder voice. "Let me comfort you, Elea." In one fluid motion, Rowan flipped me so we were facing each other, my head buried in his shoulder. I risked a peep over his back.

Kitty and Tank waited in the shadows of the hidden doorway. And beside them stood Myla and Lincoln, their armor torn and bloodied. For her part, Kitty was missing a front leg and one of her gear eyes was gone. Tank stood by her side, waving his thin arms wildly.

And he glowed bright green.

My heart leapt, and not just for one reason. Kitty, Tank, Myla, and Lincoln were alive. Somehow, they'd survived the attack at the bridge. Even better, the bird's eye spell was still working, showing me that Tank could help us somehow. My thoughts raced. I sorted through everything that had happened, my mind settling on one simple question.

My parents had given up their powers. *Where did that magick go?*

All of a sudden, the fact that Tank had a magickal aura made perfect sense. My parents power was somehow stored it inside that little Spinglet. I just needed to get my hands on him.

A plan formed.

I slowly rose to face the mechanical spider that now held us all prisoner. "I don't have much magick in me, but if I give you what I have, will you promise to free Rowan and Jicho?"

"Of course," lied the Spider-Kronos.

I shot a sideways glance to the doorway. My mind reeled. I needed a plausible reason to go over there and get Tank.

Turns out, Kitty and the others had their own plans.

For the next few seconds, everything was a blur of action. Myla and Lincoln raced into the chamber, their baculum ignited as long swords. Moving in a kind of battle dance, they swept around the room. Lincoln sliced off the heads of Oculus Warriors. As their helms fell away, the mechanical fighters crumbled in to spare parte.

Myla leapt atop the Spider-Kronos. Standing on its back, she jammed the firesword straight through the center of the metal animal. The Spider-Kronos collapsed on the floor, dead. Kitty hobbled into the room, spied the lifeless carcass, and smiled.

Myla sighed. "I do so love killing spiders."

While Myla and Lincoln had been battling, Rowan raced over to Jicho and pulled the metal cords off the child. Now he held the boy in his lap, whispering calming words as only Rowan can.

There was no such happening that I hardly noticed how Tank had toddled up to my side and pulled on my pant leg. When I finally gave him my attention, Tank reached for me like a toddler asking to be picked up.

And so, I lifted him.

The moment I touched Tank's metal casing, energy rocketed through me. Power and light infused every inch of body in a way I'd never experienced before. The top of Tank's box-like form popped open. Inside lay another moonstone. This one blazed with a familiar sort of power. Violet in hue. Hybrid magick. There was no doubt in my heart. This was my parent's energy.

They hadn't given it up.

They'd hidden it to rebuild the world.

I scooped out the new moonstone with my right hand. Every inch of my body glowed with violet power. With my enemies gone, I stepped over to the Bezel Wand. My parents lay slumped on the floor beside it. Seeing them, my heart cracked with grief. At last, they'd grown in to people I really wanted to know and yet, they'd been taken away from me. There was only one thing left to do for them, and that was place their magick into the world, just as they had intended.

The old moonstone pulsed with feeble power. Kronos said he'd all but drained it. Soon Quetum would be fully dead. The Bezel Wand needed a new moonstone, one that would feed the realm with power and life instead of taking it all away.

And I had magick that could do just that.

Raising the new moonstone with both hands, I lifted it high above my head, then brought it down on the old moonstone with all my strength. The old gem shattered on impact. The new moonstone snapped right into place. I remembered what Kitty had said about the Bezel Wand. I gripped the top of the stone and pushed down.

The wand slid into the floor with a soft click.

Seconds passed.

Nothing changed.

Then the top of the new moonstone shone with purple light. More light pulsed through the floor. Brightness shimmered across my parents. It moved over the carcass of the Spider-Kronos, turning his remnants into dust. It rolled across Kitty, and she became whole again. It went over the scrap metal remainders of the Oculus Warriors, and their many parts flew back together in a new forms, becoming clockwork animals of many kinds. My mouth fell open.

My parent's magick was healing them all.

Power spread out down the Bezel Tower, lighting up the structure with violet hues. It then moved out across the realm. Buildings reformed. Towers climbed up to the sky. The outline of the labyrinth shone brightly as well, a winding set of purple lines that connected every-thing. My heart soared.

The magick of the new moonstone—my parent's power—flowed through me in ways I never imagined possible. It shaped my thoughts and sang to my soul. The energy was so beautiful and yet, hidden within it, I couldn't escape a desperate sense of longing, the hunger to hold and own. The knowledge seeped through me and then, I saw it.

The desperate moment when they realized what they had done.

I closed my eyes and all of a sudden, it was like I was

back in this control tower, on the very day when my parents had been lured here. They realized their error and desired change, but they couldn't find the strength to let go of wanting magick. Tank toddled into the room and they came upon an idea.

Just give up the power.

Let it leave their bodies.

So they set their ability inside a new moonstone and placed that gem within Tank. And then, they locked Tank up so that the only person they truly loved and trusted could ever open him up again.

And that person was me.

A voice echoed in my consciousness. It was Rowan, calling me back to the control room of today. I let go of the moment with my parents and followed the beloved sound of my husband's voice. All the while, the feel of my parents' wanting stayed with me, as did a realization.

Now, I understood them.

The next thing I knew, I was in Rowan's lap once more, my eyes closed as he rubbed my back in gentle rhythm. The deep rumble of his voice moved through me. "Are you with us again, Elea? After you reset the control tower, you collapsed."

I forced my eyes to open, half expecting to see the vision of the past again where my parents placed their power into Tank. Instead, I first focused my husband's bristled chin. "I'm back, Rowan."

He pulled me in for a tighter hug. "I'm getting very good at healing spells, by the way. You were out for an hour this time."

A jolt of alarm moved through me. "Healing spells? Is the baby safe?"

"She's fine," said Rowan. "You're both fine."

"You're going to call her Rigby," said a familiar voice. Looking past Rowan, I noticed none other than Jicho standing nearby. He was back to his normal pale self now—no bronze color at all—and he was smiling from ear to ear. I reached toward him, and he quickly stepped up and took my hand.

"I'm so glad you're all right." I said with a sigh. As my thoughts became clearer, I noticed even more familiar faces standing nearby. There were Tank and Kitty, as well as Lincoln and Myla. All of them looked happy and healed. My parents magick certainly did its work well. And beyond them all, the room overflowed with tiny Spinglets of every animal form.

Finally, off in the distance, standing by the exit doorway, there stood my parents. A weight lifted from my bones. "You're alive," I whispered.

"Yes," said mother. "The magick healed us, but we aren't mages any more."

Father stood at her side. "Thank you for having the strength to do what we couldn't. Some beings shouldn't be tempted with power. I know that now."

Kitty sidled up closer. "Your parents have agreed to be our new King and Queen. What do you think of that?"

I grinned. "I like that idea very much."

Jicho leaned in closer. "This whole adventure has

been pretty scary, but I still want to learn how to check in gateways. I mean, if I hadn't predicted all this would happen, then little Rigby wouldn't have grandparents, now would she?"

I looked over to Rowan. We shared a smile. "You brother and I agree. We will teach you how to use gateways properly."

"Thought so." Jicho puffed out his chest. "I'm glad you agreed because I already promised Myla and Lincoln that I'd open a gateway for them to their home world."

I shook my head. "You planned that speech so you could send them home, didn't you?"

"What else?" Jicho rolled his eyes. "I mean, Myla has a tail."

Lincoln approached us and offered his hand. "Thank you for everything."

Some things need to be done while you're standing up, and one of them is saying goodbye to Lincoln. I rose and took his hand. "You're very welcome. Thank you as well."

Myla strode up and pulled me into a big hug. She broke the embrace and then looked to Rowan. "Can I take your honey for moment?"

"Absolutely," said Rowan.

Myla pulled me aside, and then spoke in a low voice

only I could hear. "Look, before we go, I have to tell you something baby-wise. Are you okay with that?"

"Yes." *I think.*

"I get your fear about inherent evil and having children. After all, I'm part demon. But, your parents don't seem inherently bad to me. They made bad choices. There's a difference. Plus, I can promise you one thing."

"What?"

"If you go into this without faith in yourself and your husband, it will be trouble. Right after I found out I was pregnant, my husband got replaced by a body double. I needed to trust that I knew who he was."

My mouth fell open. "A body double? Really?"

"Tell me about it. My life is total crazy pants chaos, honey. But what's important is this. I had to trust that I knew myself and my husband. Now, you need to do that too. Have faith in your own strength and the way you love Rowan. Can you do that for me?"

How I wished I had her optimism. "I can try."

"That's all any of us can do, really." Myla stepped back and rubbed her hands together. "Now let's get out of here before my kid eats his weight in snickers bars."

As if on cue, Jicho popped his head between us. "So, can I cast all the gateway spells for everyone now?"

Rowan stepped up to my side and smiled. "What do you think?"

I scanned the room and all the happy faces. In that moment, I think I understood what Myla was telling me. There was no knowing what the future would hold, but in this moment, I could trust in one thing. I placed Rowan's hand on my belly and smiled. "Actually, I think it's time to go home."

Rowan positively beamed. "And I couldn't agree more."

ONE YEAR LATER

I slipped on a long crimson sheath that now served as my formal gown. I'd been working on updating styles for our people. Caster women often wore scraps of leather as formalwear, while Necromancers were encased in virtual shrouds. This long dress was a way of bridging the gap, fashion-wise.

Across our bedroom, Rowan did what we called our baby-dance. He bobbed from foot to foot while holding little Rigby in his arms. Our girl loved to move. Rigby swiped at his chin; Rowan smiled. "Who's the best baby in the world? You are, aren't you?"

I leaned against the bureau and eyed Rowan from head to foot. "Are you going to the party dressed like that?"

Rowan bobbed from foot to foot. "Dressed like what?"

I stifled a smile. "Wearing your old Caster leathers with baby puke on them. This is Rigby's first official party appearance."

"What do you think Rigby?" She swatted at his chin again and Rowan fake chewed her fingers. "Num num num."

I tapped my chin in mock consideration. "You know, I think she likes the Caster leathers."

"They smell familiar to her." Rowan looked up andwinked. "And we both know she's going to puke again, anyway."

"This is true." I held out my arms. "My turn."

Rowan shook his head. He'd been keeping a very accurate baby schedule lately. All in all, my husband had figured out that my *turn taking* system was ending up with me getting far more snuggle time. He pulled the baby closer to his chest. "I'm not falling for the *ten minutes and my turn is over* routine any more. I get a full hour now so back off, baby hog."

I laughed. "I thought I was being so sneaky, too."

"You are, but I'm rather clever as well." Rowan offered me his elbow. "Shall we?"

"Let's." I wrapped my arm around his and we strolled through Jiwe La Moto. Tonight's party was the nation's very first official Celebration of the Baby. Most Caster festivals involved too much mead to be family-friendly, so Rowan and I were trying to expand the repertoire. Also, we discovered that if we invited Necromancers, then Rowan's mother's side of the family wouldn't show up. They were too prejudiced to be seen with them, so they stayed home. It really was the perfect solution to *the Zoriah family problem.*

As we stepped outside, the sun was just touching the horizon line. The jungle bristled with life and noise, as did the party clearing. There were families everywhere. And almost everyone was dancing. I counted Kade and Amelia. Quinn and a Necromancer lady friend. And Jicho ruled the center of the dance area, making up his own set of moves that involved lots of wiggling and wagging his eyebrows. And beside Jicho, there danced my parents. My heart warmed at the sight.

This was mother and father's first official visit to our realm as regular mortals instead of gods, and they seemed to enjoy playing incognito. We'd been slowly building up our relationship over the last months, and Jicho certainly enjoyed opening gateways for them to visit. Having them here tonight was a good step forward.

Rowan laced his fingers with mine. "What do you say, my love? Shall we dance?"

"What will we do with Rigby?" I asked.

"Why, bring her with us."

"Yes." I grinned form ear to ear. "Let's."

And so, Rowan, Rigby and I stepped off to join the dance, and all felt right in this world.

—The End—

ALSO BY CHRISTINA BAUER

CHRISTINA BAUER'S ANGELBOUND

The kick-ass paranormal romance with more than 1 million copies sold!

CLICK TO ORDER

CHRISTINA BAUER'S MAGICORUM

Don't miss these modern fairy tales with sass, action, and romance that *USA Today* calls a 'must-read!'

CLICK TO ORDER

CHRISTINA BAUER'S DIMENSION
DRIFT

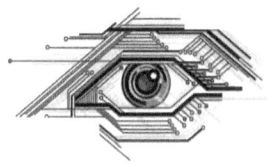

DIVERGENT meets OCEAN'S EIGHT in this dystopian adventure!

CLICK TO ORDER

APPENDIX

IF YOU ENJOYED THIS BOOK…

…Please consider leaving a review, even if it's just a line or two. Every bit truly helps, especially for those of us who don't *write by the numbers,* if you know what I mean.

Plus I have it on good authority that every time you review an indie author, somewhere an angel gets a mocha latte. For reals.

And angels need their caffeine, too.

ACKNOWLEDGMENTS

If you're reading my freaking acknowledgements, chances are, I should thank you for something. So, for the record: you are awesome, dear reader.

That said, huge and heartfelt thanks must go out to my husband and son for their rock-solid support. Writing the Beholder series meant a lot of early mornings, late nights, long weekends, and never-ending patience. You two are the best guys in the universe, period.

After that, I must thank the extensive network of reviewers, friends and colleagues who helped me build my writing chops in general. Gracias.

Finally, deep affection goes out to my late, much loved, and dearly missed Aunt Sandy and Uncle Henry.

You saw the writer in me, always. Thank you, first and last.

2. Moonlight and Midtown

3. Shifters and Glyphs

4. Slippers and Thieves

5. Bandits and Ballgowns

Dimension Drift

Dystopian adventures with science, snark, and hot aliens

1. Scythe

2. Umbra

3. Alien Minds

4. ECHO Academy

5. Drift Warrior

ABOUT CHRISTINA BAUER

Christina Bauer thinks that fantasy books are like bacon: they just make life better. All of which is why she writes romance novels that feature demons, dragons, wizards, witches, elves, elementals, and a bunch of random stuff that she brainstorms while riding the Boston T. Oh, and she includes lots of humor and kick-ass chicks, too. Christina lives in Newton, MA with her husband, son, and semi-insane golden retriever, Ruby.

Stalk Christina on Social Media

Blog:
http://monsterhousebooks.com/blog/category/christina

Facebook:
https://www.facebook.com/authorBauer/

Instagram:
https://www.instagram.com/christina_cb_bauer/

Twitter:
@CB_Bauer

VLOG:
https://tinyurl.com/Vlogbauer

Web site:
www.bauersbooks.com

COMPLIMENTARY BOOK

Get a FREE novella when you sign up for Christina's newsletter: https://tinyurl.com/bauersbooks

BEVERLY HILLS VAMPIRE

A NOVELLA BY
CHRISTINA BAUER